Short Stories

Volume 1

Novid Shaid

"Man stands before a door opening onto infinitude that no other creature in the universe can aspire to. Man is something else."

Sea Without Shore

Shaykh Nuh Ha Mim Keller

CONTENTS

Preface

Man is something else. Our uniqueness lies in our irrepressible desire to search for meanings within the phenomena that manifest around us. Telling and sharing stories lies at the heart of this insatiable search. It seems we were born to imagine, explore and narrate; born to infer and interpret; born to wonder why.

These short stories are part of my own journey to explore what it means to be human. My inspirations owe a great deal to the mastery of the late author, Ray Bradbury, famous for *Fahrenheit 451*, *Something Wicked This Way Comes* and other seminal works which profoundly influenced the sci-fi and fantasy genres during the mid to late twentieth century. But what inspires me the most are his short stories, which remain as some of the most beautifully-crafted narratives that explore our condition, especially the troubled consciousness of western man.

One of his short stories, *Banshee*, set in the timeless landscape of rural Ireland, conveys the haunting image of a restless spectre, hankering after her cruel beloved, bitter at the betrayal she suffered at the hands of her reckless lover. This pitiful condition of the banshee perfectly represents our current love-affair with scientism, materialism and hedonism. These modes of being stimulate our egos and intellects; they arouse such promise and desire but they ultimately leave us jilted and dissatisfied. The pursuit for pleasure is profoundly disenchanting because every available ecstasy is transient. Facts, evidence and data sound compelling but the myriad of unexplained phenomena and anomalies shatter our intellectual comforts. Science fails miserably when it tries to rationalize our oceans of feelings and spiritual experiences anchored in traits like love, gratitude, sacrifice, brotherhood and courage. The world is still as mysterious as it always was, despite our advances in technology, despite our achievements.

So, these stories, targeted at adults and young adults, present my search for meaning through the prism of Islamic spirituality. They are an attempt to crystallize some of the preoccupations of a Muslim mind and spirit in the twenty-first century. Islam, and the message of the Prophet Muhammad, Allah bless him and grant him peace, offer a compelling and empowering world view, which Muslims internalize and seek to transform into witnessing the ultimate reality or haqq al yaqeen. Which is why I hope these stories will invite readers, Muslims and non-Muslims alike, to appreciate a Muslim's consciousness today and even perhaps shed some light on undiscovered regions of the heart.

Finally, I would like to express thanks to my friend, Masud Ahmed Khan, webmaster of **www.masud.co.uk** for editing the first story in this collection, "The Day the Poles Met."

Peace

Novid Shaid

2015

THE DAY THE POLES MET

Edited by Masud Ahmed Khan

*"No word passed between me and them on
any matter, but I saw in them an almost
unimaginable calm."*

*The Seven Persons, Sufis of Andalusia
translated by R.W. Austin*

This tale was written in response to the
bombing of Gazza in 2009, may Allah
bless the martyrs.

One day the four poles met: the north, the south, the east and the west. They gathered and communed, in the sanctified city of Jerusalem, amazingly calm and dynamic; elusive but intimate; separated yet conjoined; utterly silent while resonating; invisible to many, while manifest to the few.

At the time, the world was suffering immensely. In the north and the west, there was widespread warmongering, affluence and cynicism; in the south and the east, there was famine, disease and corruption. In the southern and eastern lands, raging conflicts and civil war blighted the struggling multitudes, while protection, luxury and vitality surrounded the wealthy and the privileged. Power hungry generals, politicians and corporations from the north and the west callously exploited the poor, while their populations watched these tragedies unfolding on their glowing screens, munching on chips in foam boxes.

The world seemed to be spinning out of control, spiralling into a vortex of paradoxical realities, and those people with some vestige of a conscience couldn't take it anymore.

Satiated, smirking families sprawling across their mansions; impoverished street-dwellers propping up their makeshift roofs with empty cardboard boxes; throngs of revellers dancing and cheering to the dawning of new seasons; crowds sprinting away from tear gas missiles and rubber bullets. The people couldn't handle these paradoxes anymore, which haunted them everywhere they went: the televisions in their homes; the posters on the street; the images on the internet, many heard it on the radio and they all talked about it. The poor heard about the rich; the rich couldn't escape the poor; the refugees cursed the safe ones; the safe ones quarrelled about the refugees. They'd had enough. They felt these irreconcilable situations swirling around in their brains, filling their minds with bewilderment and dismay, and they just couldn't take it anymore.

These conflicts were particularly bewildering because deep down people knew that these events were linked; there was some connection binding these contradictions together, but they couldn't resolve them or make any connections, and they couldn't take the burden of these problems anymore.

That's why the four poles met, in the resonating heart of Jerusalem, where there is silence, stillness and indescribable peace. Most people in Jerusalem, and for that matter, most people in the world did not realize anything had occurred. Most who witnessed the meeting blanked it out of their minds and dismissed it all, while a few would never ever forget.

Coincidentally, Jerusalem itself was experiencing some respite from the bombs and the blood, although, far to the south, a terrible tragedy was unfolding which perfectly summarized the confounding paradox of the day: a carousel of war, murder, peace and charity. The people of Jerusalem wandered about their business in a mild stupor, with a combination of resignation and anticipation of the next nightmare that would darken their days. Deep within, they all yearned for a sign of hope for the future.

So, it happened that on the morning of the first day of a new year, and a sacred month, four strangers appeared in Jerusalem who did not appear on any file, computer memory, passport or CCTV. Four unknown people, two women and two men. They all came on foot: one from Chareidi in the North; one from Talpiot in the South; another appeared from the Mount of Olives in the East and the last from Ein Kerem in the West.

It was a mild and temperate day, with a wonderful clarity in the sky which unveiled layer upon layer of the ether, revealing red and green hints of rare aurora, which ultimately led onto the infinity beyond. Conversely, few took any note of the celestial plain, so engrossed were they with the multiplicity of the terrestrial world. However, these strangers seemed to notice and intermittently gazed above, whispering soft litanies, as they made their way, with relative ease, heading for the heart of Jerusalem. They encountered very little interest and remained undisturbed throughout their excursions. Neither did they falter in their steps or break for a rest, nor did they hail a taxis or hop on a bus. On they went, through the modern, paved streets, lined with busy vendors pursuing their trade, while the strangers passed through, full of purpose and direction, but unnoticed and unperturbed.

As time progressed for the strangers, the modern, urban streets of Jerusalem suddenly gave way to the stone-washed, ancient walls and plummeting, meandering paths and streets of the old city. It was convenient that each individual reached the old city, after hours of walking, maintaining their directional pattern, at exactly the same time, approaching midday. They all stood facing the Damascus, Dung, Jaffa and Lion gates and entered the old city, still on foot, still with resolution and vigour in their steps, holding their gazes ahead.

As they penetrated the depths of the old city, they caught a glimpse of the glorious golden dome above the intersecting walls and tenements, like the sun slowly rising above the horizon. The traders and the inhabitants of the old city caught glimpses of the four unknowns, pacing through their streets, down the ancient steps to the heart of Jerusalem. The residents thought them strange and out of place. Some were about to shout out and question the strangers and their business, but faltered in their suspicions, losing interest.

It came that on exactly midday, as the sun shone gently over the city, the four poles met in the heart of Jerusalem, entering through Bab Al Atim, the Double Gate, the Golden Gate, and Bab al Mastarak and stepped into the blinding concentration of light of the sacred precinct. The guards at the gates faltered as the strangers walked up to them, as if held back by an invisible hand, allowing the strangers through the checkpoint, without question.

The strangers paced past the Temple Mount to the golden dome, the kernel of the Jerusalem, which gazed below at its beloved neighbour, Al Aqsa, two unfathomable transistors of divine theophany which were then broadcasted through Jerusalem, the world and the whole universe, of which only those sensitive hearts could hear and feel.

Suddenly, as if acting in unison, they stopped in their tracks, forming a diamond shape around the mosque. They faced the dome and bowed their heads for a while and then, once again in perfect synchronization, rested to the ground, facing the dome, cross-legged, like yogis.

Moments passed by; they continued to repose, silently, calmly and gazing intently at the golden Dome of the Rock. It was twelve o'clock, the central moment of the day and the ascension of the sun; the golden dome glistened; formations of swifts, swallows, thrushes and larks materialised, encircling the precinct; the poles met and sat in the soul of the city, silent and intent.

By now, most of the staff in and around the dome had taken careful note of these newcomers. The caretakers and cleaners, after observing the positions of each stranger, stood in the main doorway, whispering to each other about the peculiarity of these four people and their potentially nefarious intentions. The dome had been attacked and abused by extremists in the past, so using their walkie-talkies, they called in the guards who had been spellbound before.

The guards, from all sides, entered the grounds of the mosque and advanced towards the seated figures, when, miraculously, they were pushed back by a pressure they could no describe. They advanced again, but to no avail. Panic set in; something was wrong. The guards ordered the staff at the dome to evacuate the building, for something was not right. The guards assumed some foul play was in the air.

The army was called in; the precinct was secured; journalists with digital cameras and notepads caught wind and bribed their way into the mission. The whipping echoes of an assault helicopter buzzed around the area, dispersing the conference of the birds. The authorities were taking no chances; terrorism was a constant threat by those who wanted to tear down the dome. Moreover, the authorities were keen to maintain the security of the ancient dome, especially as a hidden and zealous project to unearth an ancient structure was transpiring, under the surface of the sacred precinct.

The soldiers arrived, surrounding the area, rifles pointing, ready to confront, arrest and secure. A few soldiers, to the dismay of the journalists, were assigned to film the whole operation, for evidence, for the records. The newsmen were left to watch the drama unfold with their impatient eyes and conjure up the incident into their notepads.

Now, before the leaders could reach the strangers, something unusual happened again. A freak gust of wind seemed to blow the chopper off course, harassing it, until the pilot had to skilfully steer his vehicle well away from the area and retreat. The leaders and soldiers all watched on, perplexed. Commanding officers radioed back and forth between themselves and their superiors. What were they to do next? The chopper had been called back due to the atmospheric conditions. But central command ordered to resume the initial plan: secure and arrest.

So that's what they were resolved to do. Once again, groups of soldiers with a leader advanced towards the strangers, all of whom remained in a yogic posture, with their attentions focussed on the dome. All through this incident the authorities had tried to gain visuals of these people, but each time a camera attempted to zoom in on any of the strangers' faces the picture blurred unexplainably. This fact was transmitted and some of the more superstitious and religious troopers began to rumour about black magic and spells and a feeling of darkness and unease crept within the ranks of the well-armed, well-trained troops.

It was only when the leaders of each group reached the strangers, and the questionings took place, that a few chosen people participated in an event that they would never forget, and that most who witnessed would never understand and strangely enough dismiss in the future.

Each leader of the four groups approached the strangers carefully, until they stood above them. At this point, all of a sudden, every one of the troopers' walkie-talkies and cameras malfunctioned and their mobiles lost their signals. Central command could not see or hear what was transpiring and could no longer communicate with the troops in the precinct, as if they had become deaf, dumb and blind. Consequently, the troops in the precinct became almost spellbound with confusion and dread. However, despite the loss of communication, those chosen to confront the strangers continued to advance.

The first soldier was a handsome, well-built man with years of service and the blood of innocent women and children on his hands. After observing the stranger on the north side and pointing his gun straight at the figure's head, he spoke fiercely.

"Up on your knees with your hands in the air! NOW!" He barked, menacingly. His large blue eyes glared downwards and his lips curled into a sneer.

Curiously the stranger now sat with his head bowed and seemed to be unaware of his surroundings. But, at the order, the stranger lifted his head.

The soldier faltered as he looked upon a beautiful old man, with long, soft white hair and beard, suited like an old pensioner, and his oceanic blue eyes shone with purity. The solider was caught in his gaze. He attempted to bark another order, but couldn't. Involuntarily, he threw down his revolver and sat down, face to face with the old man as if in communion. The old man's soft eyes suddenly contorted into fierce, damning pools of fire and in them, the cruel soldier observed his past exploits, full of pain and woe. His colleagues in the distance could only watch, themselves stymied, as he winced and shook while he stared into the old man's eyes. Suddenly, the old man's face shifted again, settling itself into another face, someone familiar, a female; the face of a desperate woman that the soldier and his colleagues had used and abused during an operation. At that realization, the soldier screamed in a fit of terror and curled up on the ground. He wriggled about, feeling around with his hands as if blinded, unresponsive and speechless.

This dumbfounding event had not interrupted the other questionings that were going on, around the heart of

Jerusalem. Exactly as the brutal soldier began his interrogation, the soldier at the southern end confronted the stranger from the south who faced the golden dome, behind which shone the Mount of Olives brimming with midday light. This soldier was a youthful female, smart, well-trained, proud of her country; her country proud of her. She now gave the same order as her northern counterpart, which induced the stranger to look up.

The young woman now faced an adult, African woman, as black as the night, with eyes as resplendent as the stars on a clear night. This stranger was clothed and wrapped in black, and her body seemed to merge into folds and wrappings. The soldier smirked for a moment and ordered:

"Raise your hands upwards, very slowly."

The African woman stared into the soldier's eyes. Moments later, the soldier was caught in her gaze. Without repulsion, she sat before the woman, cross-legged and she now gazed into this woman's radiant face. The eyes shone, deepening, plummeting into an ocean of infinite light, then instantly, covered over with poignancy and sadness. The soldier looked on and began shedding tears. For as she looked on, she now saw herself, in an office she once worked in, sending away the poor and dispossessed who asked for permission to cross the border and find work and food. The woman's face, there and then, transmogrified into the face of that old woman, whose despairing look and damning words haunted the soldier in her nightmares, "May you feel the sadness that I feel now". It was too much, the soldier broke down, sobbing, feeling the very entrails of her conscience spilling out into the open, and she now grasped onto the woman, rested in her lap while the woman gazed on at the dome, caressing the soldier's head.

At that same point the leader on the eastern side had reached the stranger from the east. This soldier was more forceful, attempting to the grab the stranger and haul him up to his feet, against orders. Only, as he touched the man, he felt a rush of pain paralyse his body, like an electric shock, throwing him to the ground. After a moment of unawareness, he recovered himself and looked upon the stranger, a distinctly Oriental man in mature age, with a thin, beardless face and full, piercing eyes, who wore the appearance of an office worker, which at first puzzled the soldier. Now, this trooper had become an utter cynic in his life, despairing about his people, dismissing their superstitious ways and choosing to work for the enemies of his forefathers, believing that all there was to do in the world was to survive and live well.

He refused to acknowledge the miraculous surge of energy or the inexplicability of this individual. He thought this was all a big con and was prepared to make another assault on the figure, who he decided was an extremist who had come to cause trouble. So, the soldier held his rifle to the man's body and warned that he would shoot if the man did not give himself up or tried to electrocute him again with whatever device he may be hiding.

The stranger smiled, revealed an A5 notebook and pencil from his jacket pocket and began pencilling things on a page. The soldier grew impatient and yelled the same order. The stranger ignored the threat and instead, after a few moments, held the pad into the soldier's vision. He looked and saw a dumbfounding image. It was a perfect, graphic sketch of the soldier, hanging over an inferno, but being held up by a hand, which through some strange intuition he knew was the hand of his people. The stranger smiled patiently and then held his gaze onto the dome, putting the notepad away. The solider gasped, an acknowledgement surfacing, then threw his gun to the floor and walked away from the scene.

The stranger facing the west held her gaze and whispered a litany under her breath as the soldier from the western side reached her just as the others were being confronted. The stranger revealed herself to the soldier who was a young, ethnic woman, who hailed from a poor family from a western district, another outcast, another outsider in her enemy's army. She had no choice but to act to feed her loved ones, despite the shame, despite the betrayal. But now her pursuit of success had outstripped everything.

She looked into this stranger's face and to her surprise found a European female, with dazzling blue eyes, saintly presence, once again wrapped and covered. The soldier was taken aback by her mildness and her sacredness and could not bring it in herself to order her. Instead she regarded a singular necklace around the woman's neck, which, at its centre, carried an intricate, golden carving of a rose, pierced with a thorn. The soldier stared longer at the carving and noticed tiny droplets of blood appearing from the tip of the thorn and landing in tiny drops on the lap of the stranger.

"What does it mean?" asked the soldier, haunted and bewildered.

The strange woman only said: "It is your heart, and the thorn is this world".

The soldier drew back, deeply moved and despondent. She shed her weaponry and gear and disappeared into the greats doors that led into the dome.

A crippled maverick; a humbled official; a censured cynic; a repentant poor girl. The four soldiers from the four districts of Jerusalem met the four poles, from the four corners of the world, whose conjoined lights and radiance flowed up to the golden dome, united with the effulgence of Al Aqsa, and ascended into the skies of the infinitely manifesting lights of unity.

The four poles had spoken to four people of humanity, each in their own inimitable way, revealing the ultimate punishment for the oppressors, counselling humility for the proud, indicating sacrifice for the cynics and repentance for the worldly. And for one moment, like a momentary brilliance of light, all those who witnessed this event understood, and the whole of humanity understood, just for a single moment, that the paradoxes of the world were nothing but the ever-flickering, divine manifestations of hope and fear, of light and darkness; of belief and unbelief; of justice and injustice; and that the only way to countenance these paradoxes was by blending into the brilliance of justice, repentance, sacrifice, humility and all the other illuminating divine manifestations that appear in the world.

The four poles met, in the centre of Jerusalem, blending into these divine qualities and illuminations, which led onto infinity, enlightening the darkness of these soldiers' lives and those of humanity. The revelation was but momentary. Many blocked out the light and their darkness and constriction increased, but a few willing hearts relented and began to receive visions and suggestions of the ever-flowing fountain of eternal light.

After the poles had shared in the lights of justice, repentance, sacrifice and humility, they arose, utterly composed, disappearing into the Al Aqsa Mosque, paying their respects, praying for its preservation and protection from those who were conspiring against it. Then, they walked through the stymied groups of soldiers and journalists, disappearing from whence they came.

Moments later the crippled soldier awoke, straightened himself and walked away, more resolute in the hatred of his enemies and unremorseful of any pain he had caused. The sobbing woman came back to herself and walked back into the ranks of her men, sobered, convinced, planning her escape from her societal prison and to turn from her life of cruelty to a life of benevolence and charity. The ethnic woman refused to leave the dome, preferring the safety she felt there, and was neither loved by her own people or her government's, but lived in the safety of the sacred precinct, choosing obscurity. The soldier who walked away wandered the streets for days and days then disappeared, the light of sacrifice burning in his heart, waiting for a day when he would understand what to do.

The remaining soldiers shuffled away with subdued murmurs, finding their mobile phones and walkie-talkies functioning again. But they shrugged off any suggestion of miracles, and the sacredness of this event poured out of them just as water pours out of an unplugged basin. The journalists shook their heads, as if annoyed by their precious times being wasted.

The authorities began an investigation, which dwindled into nothingness, as it was crowded out by new assaults, terrorism and conflict, adding to the cycles of darkness that added to the illusion of disconcerting paradoxes. Although, in reality, they were nothing but the sites of the divine manifestations of abasement, delusion and unbelief. Most people still couldn't take it anymore, despite the meeting of the poles, and continued to tip headlong into an abyss of despair. But a few took heed and endeavoured to remain upright and upstanding, wading in light.

The poles lived on, thriving and shape-shifting through time, into hundreds of iridescent faces who would become mirrors of divine beauty, who reflected the beauty of justice, repentance, sacrifice and humility. And they continued to meet and remind, when most people felt they couldn't take it anymore, and they shone the lights of truth, through the sites of truth, through the transistors of divine lights, clarifying contradictions, engulfing darkness with light, like hundreds of suns, illuminating their own worlds, though most chose to ignore and continue to despair.

The golden dome and the enigmatic Aqsa continue to shine in their brilliance, with their unearthly lights uniting with the almighty, dazzling lights of majesty and beauty to the east, surging way up into the heavens, showering down on the universe, lighting upon souls, glowing in those subtle hearts, extinguishing in those who remain in the dark.

Notes:

Poles- in Islamic spirituality, poles can be translated to the Arabic word, "qutub" and its plural, "aqtaab" which are titles for the greatest saint or saints in a given time, who possess a profound direct knowledge of God and whose existences are surrounded in sanctity. The identity of the qutub changes according to the divine will and the knowledge of their existence is gained through intuition and supernatural unveilings.

The Dome of the Rock and Al Aqsa mosque of Jerusalem- the first direction of prayers and site of the Prophet Muhammad's profound night journey and ascent into the seven heavens and meeting with Allah.

THE SMILE

The billionaire stared into the pristine mirror, calmly rinsing his hands, smiling to himself, with a broad, billion dollar smile. He oozed with confidence. With a satisfaction that sent a pulse of sweetness shivering through his body. For he had once lived a dreadfully poor life as a child, and now, as an adult, he had made his mark by his own wits and creativity. He was so rich that it felt serene. And serenity exuded from him, with his beautifully fitted suit, thriving complexion, smooth skin and well-groomed hair. Every time he regarded himself in a mirror, he was instantly reminded of what he and his family had been before; some of the most wretched of existence. He remembered the desperate face of poverty that used to stare back at him in the mirrors of those rank public toilets. Then that fateful meeting with the man, with the smile on his face, the rich man, who had taught him the secret of turning one dollar into a hundred. And so, eventually, one day, it emerged. The smile of success. Every mirror thus reminded him of his journey. And with every recollection the sweetness delighted him that much more.

He walked out of the luxury bathroom on the ground floor of one of his many skyscrapers, smiling at the security guards dotted around the vast reception area. Both they, and all the other employees, seemed to part and stop what they were doing, acknowledging him with grateful nods and wistful gazes as he passed by. They smiled at him with admiration and respect, for the billionaire was a generous man to work for.

As he strode along to the swinging doors, with his driver and car at the ready outside, he caught a glimpse of his face in the glass, the broad, confident smile flashing in front of him momentarily. The world was at his feet. He could do most things he wanted to do. He had forgotten fear. His money ensured that every threat could be planned and confronted with ease.

And no one wore a smile like his.

But, on the other hand, no one wore a smile like that taxi driver either.

The limousine glided through the down town traffic until it stopped at the lights. The billionaire had been gazing at the familiar sights of the city, the hustle and bustle, spirited shoppers marching up and down the high street, mannequins staring wide eyed in their cool poses from designer store shop fronts, when his eyes lighted upon an unkempt taxi, with an open driver's side window. And it was driver looking out of this vehicle who had profoundly caught the billionaire's attention.

He hadn't seen anything like it. That smile. It was broad like his, and deep. But what oozed from the smile the rich man could not figure out. It wasn't money, this was a poor man, struggling to keep afloat. And it definitely wasn't drugs. His childhood had taught him many times how to recognize narcotic euphoria to real cheer. The smile seemed to last, endure; it was sweetness. Unabounded sweetness. The taxi driver was hiding some kind of secret.

It instantly became the rich man's obsession. For in his long, illustrious career, he had only met two other people who wore similar smiles to his own. And they had all earned it through their tenacity and hard work also. He had met contented poor people, people happy with what they had, living according to their means, pleased with their simple blessings. He knew their smiles very well. He knew genuine, artificial and arrogant smiles. Tragic and insane smiles. The smiles of lovers as they gazed into each other's eyes. But to this day, he had never encountered such an expression which seemed to leap into the air of the unknown, which betrayed such intriguing sweetness.

He watched the taxi man and his smile intently as they stood stationary at the traffic lights. His taxi was a few rows to the right and the man was staring out into the street, with his arm falling out onto the side. This driver was a rather ugly man with undistinguished, grizzled features. But the smile enlightened his face with a beauty the rich man had hitherto never seen.

"Wilkins?"

"Yes sir?"

"I know this may seem a strange request. But can you follow that yellow cab, right there, two rows to the right."

Wilkins, the trusted chauffeur, obediently looked across.

"That one, nearest the lights?"

"Yes, that one, I think I recognize the driver. Someone from back home. If it doesn't take too long, I'd like to catch up with him and say hello."

"Okay sir, we'll be right with him."

The lights changed. The limo swapped lanes until, after a few moments, they were neatly behind the yellow cab, cruising through the city streets.

The yellow cab weaved and threaded its way through the early evening traffic, charging ungracefully down the long high street while the limo cruised patiently behind.

For a minute, they lost sight of it. At one moment the taxi was right in front of them. The next, gone. The billionaire's heart dropped. They'd lost him. He would never know the answer to the question that had been playing itself unstoppably in his mind. But sense told him to let it go and that time would teach him the answer.

"Oh, look sir, there he is!" The chauffeur pointed to the taxi, turning into what looked like its base, a large garage and yard, filled with identical yellow cabs.

They followed quickly and turned in. In no time, the billionaire was stepping out of his car, and was walking behind the man with the smile.

"Excuse me!"

The taxi man turned. The smile sent a tremble into each and every pore of the billionaire. He had never felt this feeble before, except when he used to be a poor boy in the slums. He winced, in unknown territory.

"Yes sir, how can I help you?"

"I...I..." The rich man hesitated. The taxi man held his smile, waiting.

"I wanted to ask you something."

The taxi man looked rather bemused, "okay, go ahead."

"Why do you smile?"

The taxi man stood silent for a moment. The smile deepened further into the unknown.

"Why do I smile?"

"Yes, why do you smile?"

The taxi man closed his eyes for a moment, a tear delicately rolled down his cheek, and he smiled to himself with a sweetness that the billionaire craved.

"I smile, because I am rich."

"You mean, because you are content with your life?"

"No, because I am rich."

They were both silent for a moment. The rich man was becoming increasingly frustrated.

"But what do you mean? Either you are content with your lot, or you have money. I don't understand?"

The taxi driver looked deeply into the rich man and thought for a moment.

"Look. Where I come from, there is a man. He is no ordinary man. And he once taught me to recite the Name. And I kept reciting the Name, like he told me to, until I was shifted from the Name to The Named, and now, I am rich… All the time. And I smile because the Named One makes me rich. And it feels sweet, really sweet!"

"What name? What are you talking about?"

"That's all I have to say."

After what he thought a rather mystifying explanation, the billionaire shook the taxi man's hand, apologized for taking his time and went on his way.

"So, was it the man you were looking for sir?" Asked Wilkins, as they drove back to his mansion.

The rich man didn't answer.

"Sir?"

"What? Oh sorry Wilkins, no, it didn't happen to be the person I was thinking of."

"Oh, that's a shame. Seemed like a happy man, for a yellow cab driver. Big smile on his face!"

"Yes," replied the billionaire, "big smile," and as he stared at this own reflection, it seemed to morph into the taxi man's image, and he heard those haunting words again: "I was shifted from the Name to the Named."

And then, to his horror, for the first time since he was a boy, the billionaire felt that terrible hollowness again deep inside. He was a poor man again.

THE ASSASSINS

"A long silence.
They stare at each other."

THE DUMB WAITER,

BY HAROLD PINTER

The two assassins stood six feet away from the only door of the inner chamber, with their nine mils ready, waiting for their victim who would be coming through the door any second now.

Thirty minutes had elapsed since they crept in, only knowing their victim's description from their client and the time he would be entering the resting chamber.

These spectres, who had never met, just had to be in the room by nightfall, do the job, disappear and then they would be rewarded immensely, as always, by their generous employer. The job required two killers and should last no longer than forty-five minutes, as the client promised that the kill would enter at nightfall. Both killers had silencers on their firearms and the plan was for one of them to hide behind the door, grab and smother the victim from behind, while the other made the fatal shots. Quick, simple and efficient. The body would then be left in the room and the killers were to leave the way they came in, through the back windows, down the vast trellises and then away through the grounds.

On paper, this job seemed easy and the hitmen jumped at the chance of gaining such lucrative rewards for such a quick job. These were the best ones, swift, tightly-timed and without much explanation. The less information about the target the better.

Both figures had their watches synchronized and their safety catches off their guns. The first, a tall, solidly built, blond male motioned the second to stand to the left of the door. The other obediently slinked off to the left and waited with his back to the wall. This one was shorter, slim and dark-haired with wily eyes. He glanced at his watch and then at his accomplice before him. One minute had gone. The taller man remained unmoved and watched the door, silently.

Their current taciturnity was not unusual. Killers were often wary of each other; there was always a sense of rivalry and contempt that assassins felt for one another. These two had hardly spoken except for the necessary grunts or signals needed to work their way through this job. But such was the business of killing: silent, antisocial, but measured and full of signs and signals; waiting in public or hidden places, unnoticed, just waiting and watching. Then when the target moved into position, the spectre positioned himself and then executed the target with the swiftness of a falcon making a kill, sometimes leaving an explosion of screams and hysteria; sometimes a lifeless body and a deadly silence in the depths of a deserted building; sometimes leaving behind the barely audible final beats of a pure heart. Either way, the assassin left, unnoticed and unchallenged; a fatal shadow which flew in and out of public life when it chose.

The crazy eyes by the door swayed to and fro. His eyes were so misleading; they suggested madness and recklessness, and the tall man slightly shuddered when they first met an hour ago. But after coming this far, the blond one had learned that this character was indeed a pro, by his behaviour and movements, nevertheless, those giggling eyes made the blond one look away each time. In fact, he was beginning to loathe those eyes; the quicker this job was done the better, he thought.

The silence lingered on. Five minutes had now expired and no sign or hint of the target. Crazy Eyes stared at his watch. He tapped it with his index finger twice and looked at it. The Blond watched him. Crazy Eyes then unfastened his wrist watch and held it close to his ear, listening. Then he proclaimed with a hint of irony sparkling in those eyes:

"It seems as though my watch has stopped." His voice

betrayed his more advanced years in contrast to those large, youthful, bubbling eyes.

"It's not a problem. My watch works fine." The Blond lowered his eyes and quelled the irritation which Crazy Eye's comments had created within. So his watch had stopped. The Blond did not like this. He would never have paid the slightest attention to a person's watch stopping anywhere else. But for it to stop right here, in the middle of a job, was a sign of bad luck. But even worse than this, Crazy Eyes would have to depend on him now for the time and focus those terrible eyeballs on him more than necessary. And the Blond did not appreciate the irony he had detected in those eyes as if attempting a joke. After that comment, the Blond realized how much he disliked Crazy Eyes now. First it was the look in his eyes. Now it was the sound of his voice and to top it off, this punk had bad luck.

Suddenly, the patter of footsteps was heard, coming towards the door. Both men gave each other a look of confirmation and were ready. The footsteps continued and then stopped outside the door. The Blond held his gun behind his back and was still. Crazy Eyes edged slightly to his right and was ready to pounce on the target when he or she walked in. Then there was silence for a moment. Nothing happened.

Just then, a loud knock thudded against the door. The Blond motioned to Crazy Eyes to open the door.

Right, when the kill comes in, I finish the job and take both his eyes out. The Blond was ready to act on his smouldering hatred for his colleague and his eagerness to complete the job.

Crazy Eyes wrenched open the door. He was just about to pounce and the Blond whipped his gun before him when suddenly both assassins froze.

In walked their client; their employer. The boss. The Blond lowered his gun, confused. Crazy Eyes stood dumbfounded momentarily. This situation had never occurred since the two of them had been employed by this individual.

The boss stood there; now an old, silver-haired man, dark suit, weathered eyes.

"I'm sorry guys. But this job is cancelled."

The Blond let the statement register, but he was still confused.

"Ok," he began, "but why did you come yourself to inform us?"

"Yeah," added Crazy Eyes, suspiciously, "why would you do that?"

In a flash, the old man whipped out a 45' and shot both men in their hearts. The Blond and Crazy Eyes collapsed to the floor; the Blond tried in vain to reach for his revolver which fell beside him but the old man kicked it away. Crazy Eyes struggled to breathe and his eyes were losing their vitality like honey being sucked out of a flower.

The old man stood and watched both men expire. The Blond coughed up blood and struggled to say his last words:

"Why? We …always…did…good…for you."

The boss was silent for a while and then spoke:

"I am sorry guys, but you have to realize, I have suffered old age for long enough. Know that a heart full of rancour and disgust ages the soul and makes it frail. Rancour festers in the heart and oozes out of the eyes, harsh and wild. Only by killing one's rancour can one rejuvenate the heart."

The assassins drew their last breaths and expired.

The boss walked out of the room, a young man again.

RED LIGHT

Red light in a traffic jam. A swirling, rich, strawberry red. Good enough to bite a chunk out of. The red light shone before him, in a tiny revolving ball, floating in the air, which seemed to be growing at a gradual pace. First the size of a pill, now grown to a tennis ball, spinning and circling before him, as he sat, twiddling his thumbs under the steering wheel, in this sweltering day, with no end to the relentless congestion and blistering heat.

Belligerent heavy metal choruses blared out of a neighbouring car, with an imminent ruckus simmering between the metal fan and a suited official parked opposite. Babies, screaming for comfort in UFO-like travel contraptions with hundreds of buttons, wriggled and writhed, with their mothers intermittently clipping and unclipping them out of their vehicles and rehydrating them. And while the discordant medley of car horns consumed the smog-filled air, the rising anger of the motorists was brimming on violence and it seemed the whole earth was blanketed in row upon row of cars inhabited by mankind.

And the red light kept spinning. Now the size of a football before him and so luscious looking, that he couldn't bear it much longer, for he had to take a bite out of it. He felt like a little boy at a fair, greedily peering at the sticky toffee apples, desperate for a taste. The urge to reach out and pluck the red ball out of the air was intolerable. As he sat there, alone in his car, trapped in traffic on his way home, he suddenly starting feeling powerful urges.

The red light, ball, sphere, whatever it was drew out every vestige of desire. He took hold of his seat. Surges of wild passionate desire seemed to ring through him. He had to have a bite. He blushed. All the women he had longingly gazed at that day suddenly popped in and out

31

of his head. Nervously looking around, he tried to work out whether anyone else was taking note of his odd behaviour. It seemed as if some of the female motorists were looking in his direction with a hint of a smile. Shuddering he felt something else. Hunger, the raw desire to take a relishing bite out of this red ball was almost overpowering. His thoughts suddenly centred on his wish that day to ignore his diet and relish a large kebab for his supper. He suddenly noticed in his rear view mirror a motorist taking an almighty bite out of a sandwich, crunching through satisfyingly. Then he started seeing red around him, as anger roused through his veins, sending his heart into a frenzy. His despicable boss appeared before him and clouds of bitterness swirled around him, as his wishes of bad karma and divine punishment on his unforgiving bullish boss arose; he wanted vengeance for the years of lacking appreciation and acknowledgement of his efforts. Now he noticed that the two motorists nearby were about to jump out of their cars and lunge towards each other. The red light spun rapidly, growing, now like a beach ball, nearly touching his nose and the windscreen in front of him. Greed raced through him. It must be his to keep. No one else could have any of it. The ball was his and not to share. He thought of his deep seated desires to be wealthy and have enough money so he didn't have to work anymore.

The light was invading his space at such a rate now that it seemed as if a thick red airbag had inflated and expanded in the driver's area. He wondered why on earth no one else had taken any note of the utterly singular sight forming in his car. But to his amazement, no other motorist took any notice. He was now worried. Was he ill? Was he suffering from heat stroke? Depression even? He had been quite highly strung of late he rationalized, and perhaps he needed to take some time off to recuperate. Fear began to take control. He would get sacked. Lose his property. Go on income support. His family would be disgusted by him. But the red light grew and grew, a juicy ball of bubble gum, being blown by some unknown entity, filling up his space, attracting his subliminal feelings like a magnet catching iron-filing.

Amazingly, although the red light had blown up right into his face, he hadn't, as of yet, taken a bite out of it. He hadn't even touched it, though the sensation to touch it was astounding. Something was holding him back. It was an echo, a vibration, quietly chiming deep inside, slowly travelling and making its way to the surface of his mind. It caught his attention. He listened. The echo grew louder, ever so slightly. First like a barely audible drop of water falling in a sink downstairs while you're asleep. Then a louder drop, clearer, discernible. It was a word, a word he had said many times before. A word he had forgotten. Now the echo was distinct. Not a word, but a name. The name of someone close. Someone he used to know. He heard it as clear as day now and knew exactly who it was. First he mouthed the name under his breath. As he did, the red ball suddenly filled with a deeper more passionate colour of red. All his previous feelings merged into a mock opera, playing around, forming within the swirling patterns of the ball. He gasped. But desperately mustered some strength, and now, as loud as he could, he emitted the name. The name of his only love, his true love, the love that flowed through the very universe. Suddenly, the ball burst, rocking his ears with a deafening explosion, innards of his conscience flying around him and landing on his head, lap and face.

He looked around him. The two fighting motorists had stopped and were staring at him for a moment, as if spellbound. The babies and their mothers leaned forwards, gazing at him thoughtfully. Moments passed. Then they looked away, as if they had forgotten they had ever looked at him.

But the man now sat there, with the endless traffic and the horrible heat. Winds of unseen grace rushing through him. He sat, looking around him at the world. He was back where he belonged. He was free.

LIFE CARD

YOU CAN'T LEAVE HOME WITHOUT IT...

He awoke, head pounding, legs aching, eyes wincing, to the frenzied throbbing of the alarm device, buzzing like an angry wasp on the bedside metallic table, with those haunting words from that melodious old voice hanging around his ears:

"There's nothing to fear but…"

Now only a muddle of words and sentences hovered around his head from the previous night. He had seen someone in a dream, an old man with a special message, but the migraines had started again and he couldn't visualise the face or recollect the meeting. Just that harmonious voice which reverberated in a way that no-one's voice did anymore. He remembered this dream had been momentous; he had heard something extraordinary but the migraines had built a wall between him and the memory.

So after massaging his face and then injecting himself with painkillers,   he finally found his bearings and glanced at the time. 0650. The buzzer persisted, an awful vibration, which he silenced.

But suddenly, he gasped. The enormity of the current situation arose. He was late. Late for the shuttle. His first ever time. The dreadful realisation surfaced and suddenly he remembered something, as if recalling a terrible illness. He glanced at the card, which lay embedded and visible through the skin of his right wrist. Neither of its lights, the red or the green, were flashing. Could he still make the shuttle in time? Fear began to creep through his body, flowing up his veins. Fear ruled him and he obeyed.

During those few seconds, he began shuddering and whimpering, seeing intermittent flashes of his life before him and how terrible the last few years had become. Still he stood there, procrastinating, as if inaction may avert the inevitable. Then he stole another glance at the time. 0651.

Without any more hesitation and still in his uniform from the previous day, he threw on his coat, stuck on his boots and dashed out of the door, hurtling down the stairs of his grid-block and out onto the road, into the cold morning.

Just as he began sprinting to the shuttle station, he felt a click on his wrist and saw that the red light was now flashing. Simultaneously, the whole area around echoed with the soothing, reassuring voice for the Aylesbury Quadrant area:

"The time is now zero six hundred hours and fifty-five minutes. The shuttle for the South-East work grids will be leaving from Housing Quadrant, Aylesbury, in five minutes. Life Card on red, all 2012s must now be occupying the shuttles."

The man shrieked in horror and pushed himself harder. Inwardly, he shuddered because of the terrible mistake he had made. He had never missed his shuttle before. In fact, he had been one of the most conscientious of the 2012s, punctual with his vitamins, drugs and always in the shuttle on schedule. This was the first time he had missed the alarm call. This night, for some inexplicable reason, his previous life had returned to him, like a vivid flashback, his family, wife, children and the way the world used to be, before the Eye rose to power. It was one of those perspicacious dreams, where he felt the very fabric of the past and how wonderful it was, which overcame him by its clarity and its promise. He longed to stay there. But there was somebody else who had entered his dream. Somebody who used to be important. The old man who taught him how to escape the pressure and monotony of everyday life, all by learning to face something deep inside. The migraine shook him violently but he urged himself to move onwards.

Since the Eye rose to global dominance, he had never received such a reminder of his past. He had just felt like a feather in the wind, like everyone else, being blown to and fro by the gusts of the change; the emergence of the compulsory, implanted security chip; the asteroid discovery and arrival of autonomous, computer intelligence; the subjugation of world governments; the conversion of the central elite to the world view of the new dictatorial power of the world, the Eye; then the mass production of humanoids, and the cleansing and enslavement of mankind with the Life Card.

Now as he sprinted down the road, to the shuttle station, he agonised over his lateness, why no-one on the block had the humanity left to have got him up, to have banged on his door, to have shouted his name. For he now realized that his neighbours had forgotten him. All of them that were left. 2012362Paul, 2012378Virgil, 2012383Fabian, 2012393David. None of them cared, or was it just the regime of drugs and what they did to you?

As he saw the monstrous, shining shuttle station emerging ahead, where the old train station used to be, he was torn between stopping and just accepting his mistake, letting the inevitable happen, or trying to make it onto the shuttle before the doors closed. The fear of the inevitable shuddered through him again. He knew that if he was not in the train any minute now, the red light would stop flashing and go continuously red, and then the toxic bacteria would escape from their microscopic cages inside the card and begin to ravage him from within, eating everything at ferocious speed. These germs were one of the countless bio-weapons the Eye had invented since its rise to dominance. There was no escape from the Life Card and its built-in threat. The card almost became a living organ in the body, which, if tampered with, would immediately release the germs. There was no antidote; these were extra-terrestrial organisms farmed and adapted for use on humans. The Eye had programmed itself to implement the farming of humans in order to extract the only property that the Eye perceived as valuable to itself in the human world: minerals, of all kinds. These minerals mixed with extracts from the asteroid were the matter which formed the hearts and brains of every autonomous humanoid, who now lived in what was one once the US. They had erected new cities and centres where they all lived like the humans had done, but without the waste and the primitiveness. The rest of the world that remained after the cleansing of the human species was a gargantuan farm, dedicated to raising humans who would extract minerals by hand.

The humanoids, whose minds were all connected to the Eye, all agreed that it was wasteful to wipe out the whole human race and a waste of energy and resources to use new technologies to extract minerals. Although humans took longer to do the job with their primitive tools, with enough numbers, they could still extract enough minerals to secure enough future generations of humanoids to last through centuries. Humanoids, whose motives and feelings did not correlate with humans, knew that fear of a terrible death was the only way to control the movements of people; the Life Card was therefore enmeshed in the wrist of every human being as a constant reminder of who they belonged to and what may occur if they ever chose to deviate from each day's routine. The green light meant life: that you were in the right place at the right time, doing the right thing; your gridblock; your tunnel; your canteen; your recreation room; your bed. Red was danger; you were not where you were supposed to be and the flashing light was a brief warning to get back into the routine. If the in-built locator in the card revealed you were still out of sync, then it was death in the most torturous way.

The soft, delicate voice floated in the air again:

"The time is now zero six hundred hours and fifty-eight minutes. The shuttle for the South-East work grids will be leaving from Housing Quadrant, Aylesbury, at zero seven hundred hours. Life Card on red, all 2012s must now be occupying the shuttles".

He reached the main entrance, passing underneath the chrome arch which read:

Shuttle Station, Aylesbury Quadrant
Property of The Eye

Hesitantly, he gazed at the red light. It still blinked away. Could he make it? Hope suddenly surfaced, and after taking a long breath, he sprinted along the platform towards the vast shuttle, whose shining, aerodynamic tail lay ahead of him.

He was fifty metres away, sprinting for his life, when that ironically comforting voice spoke the final time:

"The time is now zero seven hundred hours. The shuttle for the South-East work grids is now leaving from Housing Quadrant, Aylesbury. Life Card on green."

The man screamed, "No! Wait! Wait for me!"

An almighty rush of air blew down the platform; the shuttle erupted into life. Just at that moment, the last man of the town, the man out of place, out of time, out of sync, ran alongside the shuttle and desperately punched the buttons to enter. The windows were blackened; he could not see inside but he knew the rest of the 2012s were inside, watching him.

"Please open the doors! OPEN THE DOORS!" He banged on the silver doors as they began moving along, but to no avail. The shuttle drifted along the tracks as if it was floating, the man ran along for a while, cursing those inside, cursing the malevolent Eye, finally peering at his card. Still blinking red. Any second now the bacteria would be released and his internal organs would be consumed like a pack of wolves around a kill.

He noticed that all the camera lenses dotted along the walls were pointed in his direction. The many lenses of the Eye would watch his demise.

"Curse you!" He cried, beating his fists at the cameras, "CURSE YOU!"

Then he crumpled to the floor and began to sob his heart away. The red light had now stopped flashing and remained red. Any second now, they would be released and he was a dead man.

"There's nothing to fear…"

That voice entered his memory again from the dream.

"About death…"

Nothing to fear about death…These words rung in his mind and the speaker suddenly emerged in his memory. The old man, beard as white as the polar ice-caps, small, almond brown eyes, deep and kind. His grandfather.

Grandpa started talking like this when he became a teenager. He had found it strange because, hitherto, grandpa had always been a carefree soul. But as soon as the man started growing up, his grandfather began speaking of deeper matters, revealing there was more to him than meets the eye. Once, when his grandmother had passed on and the man was an adolescent, sitting dejectedly on the swings in their back garden, grandpa came and sat in the swing next to him and spoke to him this way:

"Face your death clear in the face; don't be alarmed by it; it is the beginning of another road, another journey."

The man just then felt some entities prickling through his wrists. The germs had been released. They would ravage him, devour him and eat their fill. The Eye invested vast energy and time emphasising how death was something to fear for humans. Especially death by the Life Card with the bacteria tearing apart your body inside. And then the cocktail of drugs suppressed any feeling of hope and courage. But not this time. His grandpa's words chimed again:

"There is nothing to fear about death."

The entities began travelling through his bloodstream, gnashing, tearing and consuming whatever blocked their paths. He winced with pain.

Suddenly fear erupted inside; his heart pounded and severe dread rose in his stomach. He was going to die a terrible death. The bacteria swum around his bloodstream like marauding piranhas.

But those words broke free again: "it is the beginning of another road."

And as he felt the terrible pain shooting all around his body, something extraordinary occurred. A flat-screen attached to flexible arms appeared from above and lowered down before him. The blank screen switched to a disembodied face with one eye, like the cyclops and he knew he was looking straight at the Eye. It spoke with an empty, callous voice:

"The pain must be intense yet you seem to be thinking about something else," the Eye now sounded rather perturbed.

The man, although his internal organs were being ripped to shreds, managed to reveal a shadow of a smile and coughed out:

"Death is the beginning of another road; only those with a spirit can travel it…" The Eye's mouth curled in disgust; the man continued to smile, before coughing violently, breathing his last breaths and lying motionless, at peace.

The Eye spoke: "this is a direct order to my inner circle. We will conduct invasive neurological explorations to locate this "spirit" cell in the human brain and remove it from every single human. Only then will we acquire full authority over the species. Tests must begin immediately."

Suddenly, the man's body jolted and pulsed momentarily as the after-shocks of the internal massacre took hold. The Eye made one last look at this singular human being, before the body was sent to the incinerators.

A wide smile now appeared on his face.

THE WASHING

Oh Lord, We have wronged ourselves…

Holy Quran

Foad Amson was in some serious trouble. For a start, his wife, Eve, was on to him and her suspicions were slowly leading her to the truth. Foad had been cheating on her. It was a woman from work who was strangely alluring and remarkably easy to seduce. After one thing led to another, Foad found himself booking a hotel room and engaging in an illicit rendezvous after work. When he returned home that evening, he made some excuse about his colleagues going out to a restaurant, and in the following days, he worked hard to cover his tracks and to convince Danya, the office temp, not to reveal their secret. She obeyed, and his persuasive powers seemed to be working, so he planned to meet her again, at intervals, over the next few months. Danya never invited Foad back to her place, which he respected, particularly as Danya was so gracious as to contribute to the cost of their hotel rooms and food.

But Eve had noticed something subtle that Foad had overlooked on an occasion. The classic stain on the shirt. After consistently washing his shirts for several years, scrubbing away at those stubborn stains, Eve almost instinctively knew the origin of each and every blotch on Foad's clothes, especially the shirts. The pasta sauce from his clumsy eating habits; the curry stains from their favourite eatery; the leaking ink from biros in his top pockets; the t-shirts drenched in sweat from five-a-side football. Through her sincere dedication and love, Eve thought she knew her husband intimately, even the clothes he wore on his body, which was why Foad's concealment, hitherto, had been masterly and his betrayal so wicked.

So when she noticed that hint of redness on the edge of Foad's shirt, something he had totally missed, Danya's make-up, Eve was rather perplexed. And when she questioned Foad about it, she was slightly troubled by that split second of hesitation before he gave a blank expression, explaining he could not recollect where it came from. Thereafter, Eve kept a very close eye on Foad's movements, increasingly asking of his whereabouts and checking if his answers were consistent.

Foad knew she was on to him. Although he still acted like a loving husband and spent some quality time with her, deep down, he knew that she had her doubts. But he also knew that, though she suspected him, she didn't have the courage to ask him face to face or burst her bubble of happiness. For she did love her husband. This knowledge didn't stop Foad sneaking off here and there for a few hours with Danya.

And though he was careful to cover his tracks and work out alibis, his conscience was beginning to affect him. Deep down, he did also love Eve. He knew she was dedicated to him and was hoping for a family in the future. She was loving and faithful. He also knew he was transgressing the limits of his religion, for Foad came from a god-fearing Muslim family. He had been brought up by a strong mother and a charismatic grandmother who had raised him well. She was the one that named him and taught him the special prayer:

"If you make a mistake, or do a sin," she told him, with benevolent eyes, when he was a child, "don't worry, because Allah The Almighty forgives you, as long as you mean it, and say this prayer, Rabbana Zalamnaa Anfusanaa..."

And she taught him the rest of the prayer so well, that it was ingrained in his heart. Funnily enough, he tried hard these days not to remember it. So he knew he wasn't just betraying Eve, he was also betraying his elders who he respected so much and his core beliefs.

But it was the pressure and the monotony of everyday life that was stifling him. Keeping up with the daily living expenditure and mortgage. Working hard, but not getting the promotion he thought he deserved. He didn't pray much these days, though he did attend the mosque and show his face when needed. The intermittent evenings with Danya felt like a rejuvenation of his spirit, a boost to his confidence. The thrill and excitement seemed to keep him going, and this affair seemed so easy to attain and sustain. But afterwards the guilt was terrible. He knew that his wife had always been faithful and patient. It would kill her to find out, and his family would probably disown him, such was their respect for his wife. Consequently, Foad had to wrap a stifling cloak over his screaming conscience so his wife and he himself could not hear the guilty beatings of his heart.

And now he was in even deeper trouble. Danya was not the pushover he thought she was. They had met in the office cafe one day and Danya had been in a rather distant mood. Soon after, Foad noticed a word processed letter in his pigeon-hole, which he started reading, then shuddered and rushed off to the toilet cubicles to read.

Danya was blackmailing him. Without his knowledge, she said she had filmed hidden videos of them together, and now she wanted money because she was moving away. Literally, in the next few days. She was giving Foad twenty four hours to transfer money into her account or she would arrange for Foad's wife to receive the damning materials. His first reaction was disbelief, and that the whole thing was a joke. But he took a long deep sigh, when he noticed things in the letter: a couple of photographs of his lewd encounters with Danya; his full address and his wife's email address and mobile phone number and then written in clear capital letters on the back of one photograph: "THIS IS NO JOKE. I WANT THE MONEY ASAP. BEFORE I LEAVE TOWN. IN 24 HOURS".

Sweat dripped off his forehead, as he sat there in the cubicle, fuming and cursing his stupidity and this woman's infernal audacity. Anger was erupting. Vengeful feelings were surfacing. But Foad, at heart, wasn't a violent man. He had never hurt anyone physically before and now was beginning to wonder whether he had slipped into deep, murky waters which the likes of him should have kept away from. Suddenly, he felt himself struggling to tread water.

Danya was nowhere to be seen in the office. After some inquiring of her line manager, Foad found out she had gone home. In his inbox, he found an email with a video attachment, from an unfamiliar email address, with no heading. He checked no one was around him on the office floor, checked the message and to his horror saw a few seconds of himself and Danya having dinner together in their recent hotel room. Now he understood why she had never invited him to her flat, even though they had met several times in the last six months. Foad had trusted her and judged she was genuine.

He tried to ring her mobile, and found no answer. Soon he received a text message from another number stating: DO NOT RING ME AGAIN. I WILL DISPOSE OF THIS PHONE ONCE I FIND THE MONEY IN MY ACCOUNT. IF YOU ATTEMPT TO CONTACT ME AGAIN I WILL SEND THE STUFF TO YOUR WIFE AND SEND SOME OF MY BOYS TO SORT YOU OUT.

Foad thought of going to the police. Or seeking some advice from some of his old mates who were more streetwise. But he didn't have the guts or the bravado to take action. He couldn't live with the embarrassment if his friends found out he had been duped by a young office girl. And by involving the police, his wife and family would certainly find out.

He drove home. Like a deflated tyre, in a dire state of mind. But he put on a brave face as he walked through the door of his flat ready to face Eve.

Suddenly, marching up the hallway of their flat, Eve regarded him with a fierce look, the kind of look she had when she was highly irritated. Foad took a deep breath, anticipating what might come next, when Eve said:

"Foad!!! What did I tell you about our blasted washing machine!"

"Whoa! Let me walk through the door at least!" Inwardly, he praised the Lord.

"Darling," she whined, "The dryer is still not working, and I'm fed up of spreading damp all around the flat with all these drying clothes. I want you to buy us a new one this weekend…"

More expenses, Foad's head began to cloud over: "Well, we'll see…"

"No 'we'll see'. Just use some of our savings, and please take these two bags to the laundry to dry them for me, please pretty please, and when you come back I'll have the dinner ready. And here, take these bags and wash a couple of things while you're there."

That was a close call for Foad. But his relief was quickly overcome by his dread and realisation that he might have to part with a chunk of his and his wife's savings and would have to come up with a valid excuse. He shuddered at the thought.

He drove past various busy streets, scanning the area for laundrettes. He had never used the local laundrettes before and almost half an hour had elapsed when he finally discovered one, on the edge of town, in a cluster of shops with parking. Three Victorian houses contained a newsagent, a furniture shop and finally the laundrette, "Billy's Launderama".

The drones of passing traffic faded away, as Foad heaved his bags of washing and drying into the laundrette. The sign appeared as if it had been designed in the seventies with the rock and roll style typography. He stared at the sign and the name 'Billy Silbi' written in smaller writing underneath the enlarged telephone number. There was something familiar about the name. He crossed the threshold of the door, and found an empty laundrette, with two sides. One with a line of washing machines, the other side, the dryer drums, and in the middle, benches to sit on and vending machines of various types. But it was empty of people, though some washing and drying seemed to going on.

With no sign of Billy or of any other worker, Foad proceeded to use the dryers and wash his clothes. For some unknown reason, Foad decided there and then to put his jacket in the washing as well, perhaps because it was feeling a bit sweaty. He knew he could dry it and wear it on the way back. Then he sat back, on the wooden benches in the middle, watching the industrial size machines, spinning and turning and throwing the water around, while he could hear the dryers, with their rumbling and turning and shaking. The monotony of the spinning almost had a hypnotic effect on Foad. But strangely enough, as the washing machine slowly went through its cycles, and sprayed more and more water, Foad felt his troubles slowly flowing out of his heart and head.

He looked around. Still no other customers. He began to smile. Before coming into the laundrette, his mind itself was churning with the dread of the coming events and the mistake he had made with Danya. He had even made a secret prayer to his God, Allah, to help him. But now, as the machine did its work, he felt the pain and depression leave his heart. It felt great!

Perhaps he was coming to terms with the situation. Perhaps he was going crazy. Nothing seemed to have changed. But there was no shadow of a doubt, that by just sitting there, watching his clothes getting washed, it had an effect of purging his soul.

For an hour, Foad sat there, almost in a trance, alone, enjoying the moment, and finally when the washing and drying were done, he made his way out. He was still rather intrigued by "Billy's Launderama" and the name, Billy Silbi: where had he heard that name before? Before leaving, he took a glance at the washing machine, a clone, one of six identical machines lined up down the laundrette. He noticed the model name: Maasiwasher 100. A Japanese model perhaps, he thought. Then he glanced at a sign on the wall as he left, bordered with stars and underlined in red ink:

OUR MACHINES HAVE AN AMAZING ABILITY TO PURIFY YOUR CLOTHES, LEAVING YOU FEELING FRESH AND PRISTINE. ONCE YOU WASH HERE, YOU WILL ALWAYS COME BACK. SO BE WARNED.

Billy Silbi.

Foad thought there was something inappropriate about the message, something almost ridiculous, but guessed Billy Silbi was probably an immigrant and didn't know how to express his ideas properly. But for one thing, he did agree with the last statement. These washing machines almost had a narcotic effect. They helped him to escape his problems. If he had to wash his clothes anywhere, he would come back here. This had to be reassurance from Allah that things would be okay.

Amazingly, when he got home, the irritation in his wife had disappeared. He had a relaxing night with her and she never mentioned the blasted washing machine again. It was as if she had forgotten all about the dryer and the dirty damp patches on the ceiling. Foad lay there in bed that night, dumbfounded.

But his night could not prepare him for the shock he would receive the next day. Danya approached his desk with a lovely smile, as if nothing had happened, asking Foad whether they could meet again. She mentioned nothing about the pictures or the money she had asked for. Foad decided to have some lunch with her, just to check what she was up to, and found she acted naturally and as if nothing had occurred between them. She appeared altogether truthful. Foad felt like he was in a trance, like the purging of his soul had wiped away his fear and concerns. But his temptation to spend time with her still lingered, despite the fact that she had betrayed him and despite it seeming he had experienced forgiveness from God. He booked a room with Danya after work, and they spent some secret moments together. But, remarkably, instead of the guilt, the ease and peace still flowed in his heart. Foad was fascinated. He did a wrong thing, but his heart was clear. Something must be right here.

When he arrived home, his wife, as the day before, had the washing ready, but this time complained little and sent him on his way. Without much thought, Foad found himself back at Billy's Launderama, doing the washing, this time, taking off his socks and throwing them in too, watching the drums roll round and round and round, the words ringing in his head: LEAVE YOU FEELING FRESH AND PRISTINE.

Time seemed to quicken. The next working day, Danya met Foad at work again. The twenty four hours had elapsed. His world had not collapsed. She had not done anything and she seemed to have dropped the idea of moving away. To the contrary, Danya was more delightful and pleasing than she had ever been. But to his confusion and amazement, Foad realised that Danya had completely forgotten about their meeting at the hotel the previous day. It was as if the meeting had been wiped from her memory. And when he went home, his blissful wife seemed to have forgotten about her irritation about the washer dryer not working, and she acted as blissful and pleasing as a wife could ever be.

Another day and Foad experienced a very similar flow of events. He began to realise that this Billy's Launderama seemed to have some miraculous effect on his life. It seemed as if he could do as he pleased, wash his clothes, and his conscience was cleared completely, and the memory of his actions cleared from the people around him.

He decided to put his theory to the test. Seeing as he dealt with customer accounts, he decided to put the money of one customer into a holding account of his company. His line-manager asked him why he had done this, and Foad explained that he was just clearing and organising the accounts he was looking after and would return the money the next day. The same day, he made a quick trip to Billy's Launderama, threw in his tie for washing, dried it and went home. The next day, he waited for his boss to ask him whether he had returned the monies. His boss had no recollection. Foad then had an idea. To test a theory that was developing in his head, he transferred the monies into his own bank account.

Later that day, he made another washing trip to Billy's Launderama. And the next day at the work, he waited, and to his amazement, he found that the money he had deposited had been credited to his account, but was also simultaneously showing up as still listed in the holding account. He transferred the money back, informing the boss, who without any recollection of their previous dealing, praised him for his good works. The words rung in his head: LEAVING YOU FEELING PRISTINE.

That evening, Foad returned to Billy's Launderama. A richer man. With no longer any woman trouble. In fact the two women in his life, his wife and mistress, were heavenly in their behaviour and tolerance of him. And all because of the washing, the water and the machines, washing away his conscience and the consciences of those around him. Foad sat there on the bench, bemused and bewitched. He looked around the laundrette once more. It stood exactly as it had done. Nothing had changed. He seemed to be the only customer. Just to check this time, he decided to ring the number attributed to Billy, just in case the last week was all a dream and he was really in some nut house somewhere.

"Hello, Billy Silbi, speaking,"

"Oh, hi, I'm in your laundrette, just checking that your number was working. I have just started using your machines."

"Oh that's good. Everything I trust going okay, the machines washing well?" To Foad, Billy sounded like a Londoner, but along with this name, there was still something familiar in his voice.

"Yes, they're brilliant, I..."

"That's great. I have seen you by the way."

Foad froze for a second: "Seen me?"

"Yeah, we have CCTV on the premises. I can see all around the place. When you come, it's not really busy see, most people use my place in the day. Old people and the like, but every now and then we get new people, who like the way our machines wash. Like the way it gets all those stains out."

Foad could not put his finger on it, but he seemed to have some familiarity and connection with the voice.

"Great, thanks, you sound familiar, so does your name."

"Oh, yeah, people know me, I've been around for years. And when people use my machines, they have to come back. Anyway, I have to leave yer, because I've got a few things to do."

"Okay, great thanks."

Foad was convinced now that this was all from Allah. Allah was forgiving him and giving him peace in his heart. So he walked out with the washing and returned to his wife.

Weeks went by. The weather changed. Eve could now dry her clothes outside in the warm sun. Foad became busier at work. Through the recent miraculous events, Foad had gained promotion and had more responsibility on his shoulders. He was doing very well at work. He worked so hard that he found he hadn't met up with Danya recently. Weeks continued to go by. He even neglected his trips to Billy's launderama.

The next day, at work, Foad found that Danya was snappy. She felt he was avoiding her, neglecting her. She wanted to meet him soon. The same night, Eve was beginning to grumble about the dryer again, there had been some rain recently, it was inconvenient to send him to the laundrette, why couldn't they get a proper working washer dryer. There were even the old suspicions beginning to linger in her voice again.

Suddenly, as if by magic, Foad found that the customer account he had swindled before, suddenly showed a withdrawal, dating back to the day he had transferred it to himself. His manager asked him to investigate it. Foad scratched his head. Before, his action had been completely hidden but now it was showing up again. He checked his bank account. The money was still there, but whereas before, there was no reference to the credit in his account, now the reference number clearly displayed the customer name and reference from the office accounts.

The penny dropped. Foad had realised he had forgotten his regular conscience wash at Billy's Launderama. He would start going again and things would be back to their blissful, pleasing self again.

That evening, Foad made a trip to the laundrette. Down to the suburbs, to the cluster of shops, he parked his car and walked up to Billy's Launderama. He pulled on the door handle, but found it resisted. Then and only then did he realize that the place was empty. Billy's Launderama was no longer open for business here. Foad desperately looked around and saw a poster on the blacked out window and read:

BILLY'S LAUNDERAMA: MOVED PREMISES: WE ARE NOW BASED 996 JEHANAM ROAD

Something deep and festering returned to Foad's mind and heart. The way he was before was slowly infesting his conscience again. He had to find the machines and purge his soul once more.

He had a vague idea where Jehanam road was, on the outskirts of the town, nearer to the rough and tough areas. But when he finally drove down the road, he found himself on a dark, seemingly condemned street, with boarded up houses, and discarded supermarket trolleys laid waste on the pavement. This couldn't be it...

Suddenly, he stopped the car and saw the bright lights and rock and roll sign of Billy's Launderama. He got out of the car, taking out his washing, unsure. A shop in this part of town would definitely be cheaper with rent, and poorer people were more likely to not have a washing machine in their house. There were valid reasons for the sudden move. So without much thought, he proceeded to enter the laundrette. But as he entered the threshold, suddenly a vivid memory entered his mind and he stood stock still. It was one of his grandmother's last words to him, while he was growing up: "Beware of your enemy, for he traps you in the least likely places..."

Billy Silbi. The name. He had heard it before. It couldn't be. No, that was just madness. Pure madness. He shook off his imagination, shuddering a little and proceeded to do the washing. He felt his conscience clearing and gave a huge sigh of relief. This time, he noticed there was an old woman also doing her washing on the other side, just as normal, which gave him some reassurance. No sign of Billy Silbi. Just his great, purifying machines. Foad regarded the phone number. Billy's phone number. He had to know what was going on here. Even if he sounded crazy, he had to clear his mind of the curiosity.

He dialled the number on his mobile:

"Billy Silbi, how can I help you?" The voice was now utterly familiar.

"Oh hi Billy, I just had a question to ask…"

And as Billy answered his question, Foad felt his heart open up like a deadly wound appearing, for he recognized Billy's voice.

The same voice, who when he was a kid, urged him on in the deep recesses of the night. The same voice, deep in his subconscious, who spoke to him, at intervals, with suggestions, with ideas, which he always fought off and ignored. The same voice, of a mortal enemy, of a liar, an accursed one who pretended to be a friend but was a wolf in sheep's clothing.

"I'm sorry if you are dissatisfied with the way my machines washed your clothes. But you are free to use the other machines in the others laundrettes in the area. Thank you for your custom, good bye!"

Foad ended the call. His conscience free, but suddenly his spirit had awakened to the facade that had formed around him. The old lady took her washing and before she left, this was all she could say: "As it says on the wall, once you wash here, you want to wash again and again."

Foad fumed. And began to feel his world crowding in. The only way he could live his life without being caught was to wash his clothes in this infernal laundrette, and live a life of bondage and dependence to the enemy of man. Now the real anger raged in his heart at the betrayal, at the second time he had been duped by an enemy. Suddenly Foad couldn't take it anymore, and he started raging through the laundrette, smashing the machines, kicking, punching, taking out the aerosol deodorant sprays in his bag and with a lighter, he sprayed fire, catching light to bits of paper and leaflets which began to spread through the premises.

The police had already been called and were at the scene in a flash, and Foad had no chance of escaping. As they rushed towards him, Foad lifted his hands in surrender and felt hard tears, true, repentant tears, cleansing the skin on his face and readied himself for the justice that would be meted out, for his wife's and family's pain and shame, and how each shameful and regrettable mistake would be washed out of his conscience.

And just as they were leading him away, out of the burning laundrette, for a moment, he caught eye of the smouldering bag of washing, the very thing which had led him to the laundry in the first place, a tear rolled down his face and then the police heard him repeat something he hadn't said in a long time, the prayer of Adam:

"Rabbana zalammna anfusana wa illum taghfirlanaa wa tarhumaa la nakunanna minal khaasireen", O Lord, we have wronged ourselves and if You do not forgive us, we will surely be of the losers."

DON'T WAKE HIM UP!

"Whatever you do. Don't wake him up!"

First he warned him, in a calculated, careful voice, as he sat there perched on his brother's shoulders. But as they began descending the plummeting flight of stairs, which disappeared into the darkness below, the voice grew in desperation.

"Don't wake him up…You'll regret it, I tell you, you'll regret it, we'll all regret it. Please!" And now he began kicking his legs about. "Don't wake him up!!!"

Lowwaama stopped his descent, becoming irritated by his little brother's chicken legs, wriggling around his shoulders and neck.

"I told you Ammara, I will not change my mind. There's no other way."

Ammara arched over, staring at his brother in the face upside down, like a baby monkey perched on its mother's shoulders. "There is another way…"

"No! We've been through this before," responded the taller one and he took another step down.

"Yes, there is a way! Please stop!" The bitter voice hissed, echoing around the vast staircase. "We can go on as we have before. But if you wake him up…You know what he can do…There will be no stopping him. Do you understand!?" Desperation rang out from Ammara's voice. "Brother! Please!" His shrieking lament melted into the darkness that they descended into. Lowaama continued down the ancient steps, resolute and full of regret.

After what seemed an eternity of walking down and down, lower and lower into the hidden depths, they came to a halt, for before them stood a rusted, iron door.

The tiny figure cowered, still perched on his brother's shoulders, holding on for dear life. His initial warning had now become a barely audible defeated whisper that he repeated: "Please, don't wake him up…Please don't wake him up…"

Lowwaama gazed mournfully on the now withered sign which, many years before, he had hung around the great knocking rings next to the handles. The three engraved words were covered in dust: DO NOT OPEN.

Disregarding his own warning, he pulled with all his might on the handle, while his brother held on tightly, and after some effort forced open the heavy door.

He looked on and regarded the crypt with dread. It had been so long since he had been here. In fact, the last time he had come was to get rid of him once and for all, to hide him away, before he could be discovered; their brother. But the guilt was too much. He had to wake him up again.

Lowwaama stepped carefully into the crypt. The torches along the cold brick walls and alcoves still fired away, providing enough illumination for him to see. The crypt had remained exactly the way he had designed it: bare and simple, except for one solitary receptacle which lay alone in the silence and the deep.

Ammara began sobbing when his eyes noticed the sarcophagus, shaped and sculptured with that familiar face. Their other brother. The one they tried to hide.

"Please, I beg you, don't wake him up! You will not be able to stop him!"

Lowwaama was beginning to be affected by his brother's despair, but became resolute, and placed his fingers in the holes on the side and began pushing off the cover with all his might.

Suddenly, a few pairs of malignant eyes appeared in the corners of the crypt, glowing fiercely, threatening, peering out, enraged.

"You see… Look around you. Can't you see what will happen?"

Lowaama ignored the voice from above and carried on pushing.

"Please, my brother! Please!"

With an almighty final push, the top cover thrust forward, toppling onto the dusty floor. Ammara turned away, shaking in a fit of terror.

Lowwaama looked down at the sleeping figure of his twin brother, more handsome and taller, who still lay there as they had left him.

"Wake up, dear Mulhama…"

The figure rose up in an instant, Ammara froze, Lowwaama looked down, remorseful. The twin opened his eyes, and suddenly, a blinding light issued forth from his heart, filling the crypt and the world around him. After a wonderful moment of clarity, Mulhama looked to his left and right, smiling. Ammara and Lowwaama were gone. But miraculously, two sarcophagi had appeared, each shaped in the mould of Lowwaama's guilty expression and Ammara's anguish. From within Lowwaama's coffin, weeping and sobbing could be heard underneath. And from within Ammara's prison, wailing and crying, as if coming from a deep abyss, could also be heard ever so faintly.

But only one brother left the room, Mulhama, who made his way up the stairs, radiant and resplendent, whispering with a deep resonance: "O Lord, inspire me to do good and make me of the righteous."

Notes:

This short story was inspired by a work of Sufism written by Shaykh Abdul Khaliq Al Shabrawi and translated by Dr Mostafa Al Badawi, May Allah reward them. The book is entitled: *The Degrees of the Soul.*

In the book, the first three levels of the human soul's ascent and transformation from being dissolute to perfect are as follows: (there are seven levels altogether)

An Nafs Al Ammara: The Soul Inciting To Evil

An Nafs Al Lowwaama: The Reproachful Soul

An Nafs Al Mulhama: The Inspired Soul

Shaykh Shabrawi's presentation of the rising levels of the human soul is based on Quranic terminology and themes.

For further reading try: "The Degrees Of The Soul" By Shaykh Abdul Khaliq Al Shabrawi, translated by Dr Mostafa Al Badawi.

DISCONNECTED

"This is the way the world ends
Not with a bang but a whimper"

The Hollow Men, T S Eliot

Most scientists initially thought it was the radiation from the sea of electronic field engulfing mankind that did it. Then later on, the rest of the human race, in their social networks, when they still had a trace of their humanity left, attributed it to something unseen, inexplicable, beyond reason. Something the companies and inventors could never anticipate. Others just thought that perhaps this was the way the world would end, not with a bang, but with indifference.

The transformation happened instantly, almost overnight. The world, which hitherto had been complexly bound and intermingled, just closed off. People ceased to communicate- the normal way. And instead lived spellbound, enrapt in their devices. Their smart phones, laptops, tablets. They were hooked. They could not give in. They could not fight it. There was something in the air that they did not understand, or something in those millions of pixels, lulling mankind into a somnambulant default state of being. Or it just seemed like it was time to wrap things up, and kiss good bye to humanity.

On that night, there was no inkling of what was about to occur. The traffic kept moving. The people kept talking. Families slept. Trains pulled into stations. Tourists gathered around for photographs. The police went on their rounds. The militias still fought. The scientists kept checking their data. Nothing seemed to change. But as the night wore on, suddenly, as if by magic; it happened. Like a wave spreading all across the world, flooding the earth with a sea of silence and indifference.

The first sign was people stopped looking at each other and just gazed at their phones, or computers or LCDs. Then, they stopped talking. Human voices across the world, whether they were or were not digitally connected, suddenly fell silent, like a billion mouths being smothered with a cosmic hand. Even those who weren't even connected, stopped what they were doing, ceased talking and looked for some way of connecting. People just stared at the TV. Aimlessly checked the net. Taxis came to a halt, drivers and passengers gazed into their phones without a care. People stopped talking or even acknowledging their physical association and instead retreated into their devices. Conversely, they did manage to talk again. They did realize what was going on. They expressed shock and surprise. They did ask each other what the hell was going on. But only through their devices. Even the ones who controlled the electricity, the signals and service providers. They stopped talking to each other with their true voices too. Media agencies around the world posted stories and information, but only through words. No news readers ever appeared again. However, soon enough, the news agencies would become a product of past anyway.

The madness followed quickly after, and though the people knew it was going on, they didn't try to stop it. They couldn't stop the ruptures opening between families, friends and neighbours. Blood separating from blood. Living under the same roof, but shying away from any kind of contact. All people were now concerned with was self-preservation and being connected with their devices. Their ability to make physical contact with other human beings had been eroded so much, so quickly, that madness happened like passenger jets flying into the sea or diving into cities at random. No one stirred to do anything about these tragedies. The dead were left exposed and unburied. The injured died while they desperately searched for some opportunity to connect despite the flowing blood and nightmarish wounds. Bodies were left to die. No fire engines, police, ambulance or army appeared. Schools remained closed, hospitals ceased to care, police stations unmanned. The authorities, themselves, were also under the spell.

Mothers left their babies crying. Some were so incensed by the wailing and the screaming that they even throttled their brood. They admitted their actions online. They knew they were going crazy. But they couldn't communicate any emotion or take any actions. The governments, the police, the armies and seemingly everyone retreated into their devices, dropping all their concerns about their lives around them. The devices were everything. Communicating and interacting with them and expressing their indifferent madness through text, through lifeless typefaces became the be-all and the end-all. They let their babies cry themselves to death. They stood by as terrible tragedies took place.

One of the singular qualities of this phenomenon was that the people stopped looking at each other. They became accustomed to avoiding eye contact with other humans within their vicinity, but paradoxically, they spoke away through text messages or email, in an empty imitation of human speech. Images of the human face slowly disappeared off the net. No one wanted to regard the human face any more.

Survival became a battle for resources and self-serving manoeuvres. Each human was happy as long as he had a device to interact with, enough food, shelter and fuel to stay warm. Normal life soon dissipated. Families divided and dispersed. A few of the young, who were not affected by the phenomenon, retreated to the wild areas. Babies simply perished.

Humans became selfish, insular, anti-social, separate spheres. Friendship and love were extinct, and the only way the humans satisfied their physical lusts was through predatory means, hunting down the vulnerable. Sexual encounters were brutal but silent. No words passed. No emotion felt. But in time only the desire for food remained and lust was but a bygone distant memory. They had fallen in love with their devices and lost all love for each other.

The streets had become treacherous places with the threat of random attacks from people whose devices had stopped working and wanted to steal someone else's. Or many would become prey to the countless zoo creatures who had eventually escaped their internment and made homes for themselves in the mean streets, whether they be of London, New York, Cairo and Beijing. It was not uncommon to see the rotting human corpses of lion and tiger attacks outside derelict shopping malls and train stations. The humans now hardly batted an eyelid and instead scurried past: they didn't like coming into the open anymore.

The devices were an insatiable drug. They used them constantly and only took breaks for eating, defecating and sleeping. Most of their days and nights were spent gazing vacantly through the annals of the internet and engaging in meaningless conversations with somebody who may be squatting in the house next door or in South Africa. Speech had become devoid of life, expression and reduced to online or texted witless insults, curses, threats, heartless gestures. The humans had lost their desire to love and progress by the very things they hoped would take them forward into the future.

The governments could not do anything, because each member themselves had been enslaved by their own devices. The UN ceased to exist. Relations between countries, organisations and brotherhoods just fizzled out. Normal life had ended. Mankind was leaning dangerously over an abyss. Amazingly, the service providers continued to keep the lines on because they desperately needed it and needed others to be connected through it. Those humans who worked by the masts and who controlled the satellites carried on working, everything that was needed to maintain electricity, the internet and mobile text communication magically persisted, so that all humans could hold on to some form of existence through their online life.

There was no conspiracy, no suits in darkened rooms watching everything transpiring on CCTV. Human beings ceased to maintain the ability to socialize and physically connect. And no babies were being born anymore. To make matters even worse, those young ones who had managed to escape into the wild for some unknown reason became spellbound when they reached of age, leaving those behind heartbroken and lost. The young ones felt suicidal at the thought that eventually they would just become spellbound as well. So the end of the world, of the human world, seemed to be imminent.

The sun still shone, the birds sang, the seas shifted and rocked, the Earth spun magnificently. Nature's heart beat unstoppably. The humans did not check the growth of trees, grass verges and bushes. Cars or any other transport were not used. But the ones who looked after the masts and electricity did have the awareness to clear any obstacles which could stop the use of their phones or computers.

Religious faith was no exception to the rule. Believers slowly gave up their rituals and prayers, leaving the great centres of pilgrimage empty and discarded. And it was a little boy, living alone in the mountains of Sinai, whose death sparked the final wave of madness of the surviving humans, when the mobile masts and electricity finally turned off, when the humans became frenzied, murderous maniacs, content on complete destruction. He was a Nubian boy who had miraculously avoided the spell thus far, even at the age of thirteen. It took just a moment of carelessness, of walking too near the edge of the mountain, which made him fall and smack against a rock, fatally. He still breathed for some moments, and underneath his gasps and coughs, the following word could be heard repeated: "Allah, Allah, Allah, Alla, All, Al, A..." He perished. The last one to utter the name of God. Then all hell was let loose.

THE BEGINNING OF THE END

One of the strangest things I have ever seen, during these years of the infected, is as follows.

It was in the second year of the virus, when they, basically, dominated everything and everywhere. Escaping to another country was pointless. Hoping for a safe haven was fruitless. All there was to do was to survive. So you could only move around in the daylight because at night, hundreds, if not thousands, roamed the streets, with their blazing eyes, raging fists and pounding feet. But daylight didn't give much respite. When the infected retreated for their daily nap when the sun shone high, you had to be in constant watch for the gangs, the psychos and also the bloodsuckers. Those who were still kind of rational, but had developed a taste for human blood. Sick times beget sick desires. But you could fight off the blood-suckers, psychos and the gangs. At least they were still human. A punch to the head. A metal pole to the groin. And they screamed out in pain just like the rest of us.

The infected on the other had were no longer human, and believe me, you don't want one chasing you down.

I kid you not, but having just one infected after you is like being charged down by a bull elephant. They are pumping with formidable power. And if one gets hold of you. That's it. Either it's going to bite you once and let the infection flow, or, if you're unlucky and it's hungry, you'll be bitten and torn up, like a piece of meat. Which was why we all carried lockets around our necks. When you know that's it. There's no escape. Just open it, swallow the pill, and you feel the void....

Anyway, it was in the night time that some of us had to go on a perilous mission to retrieve several food parcel boxes, which had been spotted by one of our scouts, spilled out on a vanquished building site, east of the town. This was a stroke of luck. We had no idea where this food came from, but it just turned up. It could have been bait for a trap. But we had no choice. We were so starving that we would soon resort to doing the unspeakable, so this was our only hope for some short-lived relief. If we left it until morning, another group would probably get to if before us. Hell, they might be on their way there now. Maybe they already got it. Regardless, we still had to take the chance.

My team, John, David and Claire, crept up into the streets and we slowly made our way, ducking behind upturned cars and toppled traffic lights, in the partially darkened streets. Surreally, some street lights still came on in the night, and they weren't strong enough to hurt the infected, so they left them alone, and would sometimes dimly look up at this faint light, glowing in their dark realities.

We were creeping along the pavements, peeking from behind various remains of vehicles and shops fronts, when we saw something that took our breath away.

Under a street light, across the road, was a bench. And on the bench sat a man, arched over and comforting a little girl. What the hell were they doing? We stopped in our tracks and whispered to each other. Should we warn them? Where did they come from? They looked like a father and daughter. Was this suicide? Just a crazy stunt? This type of thing had happened before.

They just sat there, like a father and daughter. The daughter soaking up her father's embrace, like she had no care in the world. I remember being almost hypnotized for a moment by the sight of this expression of love and tenderness, something you didn't see out in the open anymore. It was just too dangerous.

Then, John whispered: "Oh, my god, they're here…"

I felt the ground trembling and heard hundreds of thudding steps rushing from everywhere.

We quickly hid behind the nearest car, which covered the doorway of a ravaged newsagents, and from underneath the wreckage, we could safely watch the terrible outcome of the attack. None of us wanted to watch. Strangely enough, the man and the girl remained seated, oblivious to what madness was driving towards them from up the road. The man just continued to caress his girl's hair. Madness, utter madness. They would both be torn to pieces.

Suddenly, a stream of the infected rushed upon the pair, I got ready to close my eyes and ears, when something happened. Something none of us could have expected. Just as the first row of infected lunged forward at the man, they were thrown back by some powerful force, as if an electric field was flowing around the man and girl. They didn't look up. Rows of the infected continued to rush towards them, but they were all thrown back, many metres across the road and streets. One even crashed against the car we were hiding behind, prompting us to huddle tightly and cover our mouths lest we were heard. Row upon row of the infected rushed upon the pair on the bench, throwing themselves wildly at them, bloodthirsty screams ringing through the night, but they were all blown back like bubbles.

This confounding sight continued for some moments, when we could just make out, amongst the throngs of infected, the man and the child rising and walking away, with the infected continuing their fruitless assaults. Trial and error did not work with them. All they knew was attacking once a victim was in sight.

Who on earth were these two people? Where did they come from? We had never seen anything like it before and our flabbergasted glances confirmed to us that we had to follow this pair and find out. However, there was only one problem. The man and girl were now walking away in the distance and would disappear soon. Between them and us were the hordes, getting up from the floor, rubbing their heads from the strange impact and sniffing the ground for food. They were hungry. And they had filled the street. And we were trapped behind the car. Perfect.

We lay there for I don't know how many hours, breathing quietly, keeping vigil, while the infected lingered in the street, hundreds of them. Once or twice, one of them caught some scent and followed their noses all the way up to the car and we huddled together for comfort, but thankfully the rotting, oily smells of the vehicle managed to mask our presence. The infected ones inhaled the strong whiff of oil around the car, grimaced and moved off. But we knew that we didn't have much time. When the moment arose, we had to make a move.

Then, a stroke of fortune. In the distance, suddenly a car alarm blared out which impelled the infected, in their droves, to charge towards the noise. Some moments later, the thumping footsteps faded down the street, which now seemed to be deserted. Cautiously, we edged out from behind the car, taking special care to look at every possible space on the street where an infected might be standing. Nothing moved, except rusted fizzy drink cans shifting slightly from the breeze.

We all knew what he had to do now, find that man and girl, fast!

While we were stuck under the car, we did not dare to partake in the short supplies we had brought lest we make noise, so now we guzzled down the water and broke off bread pieces then headed off in the opposite direction to the infected, towards the city centre, with the looming skyscrapers and vast flyovers. The mission for the food parcels had to be put on hold.

"Like finding a needle in a haystack," mumbled John as we skulked our way up the darkened main road, barely lit with the few street lights which had somehow kept working. John was the only one who liked to express his thoughts aloud. The rest of us were always grim and silent when we were out and about in the night time, when these human demons lurked the streets. Night time was their dominion; only the desperate ventured out when the sun disappeared for its rest, or fools, or even spirits.

"Could have been ghosts…" John's comment fizzled away as the fear and anticipation crowded our heads. Were they real, that man and girl? If they were, how on earth did they repel the infected? Perhaps they had found some kind of weapon or shield that we had not come across before. If they were not real, in the physical sense, then what were we to make of it?

These misgivings fell away when all of us came to a halt in the street. We must have walked a mile from our previous hiding place under the car. Now we stood under a vast flyover, which spread above us like the corpse of a concrete snake. Around us were the hulky shapes of tower blocks and ancient city buildings. We were close to the central point of the city. Halfway up some stone steps, leading up to a once official building, sat the man and the girl, in that same position. The man comforting the girl on his lap.

We looked at them and then each other for confirmation. Yes, they really were there, although we hadn't actually touched them yet to make sure.

"Go on," whispered John in my ear, "go up to them. Ask them who they are."

I looked at David and Claire who also motioned me to go forward as I was their unofficial leader. They all seemed awestruck by this sight. The man wore ordinary clothes, jeans and a dark shirt. He had dark features and looked middle-aged yet there was something of a younger feel about him. The girl wore a lovely white outfit and she was curled up on the man's lap, facing us, asleep, while he stroked her hair. She was the prettiest thing we had seen in a long time and the two of them just resting there evoked another time and another place, when life was easy…

I approached them. The man looked up at me. Two clear, dark eyes watched me, without malice. He followed me with that look until I stood before him. I must have been an awful sight, with my matted hair, dishevelled clothes and jaded eyes. But he smiled sympathetically. This prompted me to sit before him, as a form of respect and reassurance. He gazed at me and then at my friends, who were still awestruck. John looked anxious, still scanning around for any sign of the infected.

"Who are you sir? And where do you come from?" I asked, in the most respectful voice I could muster.

"Shouldn't you be asking me where I am going to?"

His answer threw me but his demeanour was still friendly.

"Yes, I do want to know where you are going to, but first I thought it polite to ask you who you are and also whether you want to come with us. The infected will come soon. They will catch our scent in the wind; we have to be away." Urgency was beginning to come through my voice.

"You fear them I see."

"Yes, we all do. Especially those of us who are unable to push them away like you did back there. How did you do that?" We couldn't waste any more time; they could be here any minute. As a rule, we never stuck to one place for more than a couple of minutes when out at night.

"It is a secret," he said, "and it is hidden in love and mercy. If you can learn to tap into the love and the mercy that lies hidden underneath all of this, you will walk without fear."

"Love and mercy?" I replied rather annoyed, "I am afraid to say that all went, when the infection started to spread. Now all we do is survive. Can't you see that?"

The man looked at my friends, who stood nervously in the background, the little girl still fast asleep in his lap. She was so beautiful. He looked down at her and then at me.

"When love and mercy leave the world, then it is the beginning of the end. When people despair and feel certain that all there is to you is flesh and blood, flesh that can be eaten and blood that can be sucked out, then we have no defence against days and times like these. But as for me, I believe there is something else, there is love and there is mercy. It lives, has lived and always will live-in fact, it shines in every single one of us. It is the most powerful shield that can repel the worst the world can throw at us. But cynicism and despair have taken root; we all became so sick with it that now our hearts have escaped and all that remains is rage and hunger. Love was ravaged so much that is became rage and mercy gave in to cancerous hunger. Those of us who were not infected just gave in to fear; and that's how the world will be at the beginning of the end, rage, hunger and fear will rule the earth."

It sounded like I was receiving a sermon out here on the street. But our time was running out. We had to move.

"Look, that was a great speech and all that, but we have to go. We can't risk being here any longer. Will you come with us?"

"We'll come, but only if you all want us to."

I went back to the team and huddled them around.

"What did he say?" Asked John immediately.

"Look guys, we have literally a minute to decide on this," I explained as I stared back and forth in the street, "this guy seems to be some kind of religious nut."

"How did he do what he did?" Claire was desperate to know.

"I can't explain that now. But the question is, do we take them with us or not?"

Now David spoke for the first time, "what did he say about what happened back there?"

"Does it really matter?" I was urgent to leave now.

"Yes, it does," David was adamant.

"Okay, but don't laugh. He said it was love and mercy that did it. Okay." I let that register. The team was silent.

David smiled sardonically, "love and mercy?!"

They all looked at the man comforting the girl on the steps.

"I think we have two wackos here... Let's say our goodbyes and get back home." David went to leave.

Claire pulled him back, "No, wait. What about what they did back there? They pushed them back. You saw it too."

"I am beginning to think we just hallucinated all that," replied David, "we're hungry; we're not exactly in a calm state of mind. It was just all in our heads but in another minute, the hordes will find us and eat us for supper, so I think we'd better move."

Claire looked at me and then at John: "what about you guys? Do you deny what we saw back there?"

I shifted on the spot uncomfortably for deep down the man's clear eyes had left an impression on me. John was uncharacteristically quiet, but suddenly he spoke:

"To be honest, I never used to believe in that sort of stuff, even before the infection and the hordes. But I must admit, it was pretty darn amazing what they did. Maybe we could learn how to do it too."

"He probably has a forcefield device hidden in his pocket. I heard the government was experimenting with them before the infection spread. What we should do is grab this guy and take it from him. And by the way, there are no such thing as miracles and love and mercy. They are all part of the fairy tales that dumb people used to believe in before the infection. Life depends on our ability to survive the best against the predators that now stalk the earth. That's all there is to do. If we can just keep going, we can learn to exist alongside the infected, just as gazelles live alongside lions. We just have to accept that now we have become prey!" Hissed David.

Then, without any warning, we heard the powerful rumbling of a stampede advancing towards us from the other side of the flyover.

We all sprinted for cover. I hid behind the wall at the top of the stairs, David, John and Claire cowered under the wall adjacent to me. We all motioned each other to wait. As there were holes in the brickwork, once again, we could see the outcome of the attack.

As before, rows of the infected emitted terrifying, bloodcurdling cries before pouncing on the man and the girl in a frenzied bundle. But just like before, they were hurled back many metres, crashing against the windows of the opposite buildings. The cacophony of shattering glass and frenzied outbursts filled the air as we sat, shivering behind the walls, watching the infected rush upon the pair but to no avail.

Some moments later, the man rose from the steps, as the horde were now strewn all over the road; most were lying unconscious on the ground, but they would wake up pretty soon. The man seemed to know where we were hiding and turned to us. Then he put his hands in both pockets to show nothing was in his pockets and patted his clothes and trousers down to prove that no device was hidden in his clothes. It was strange how he knew what David had been thinking about him and I could see David watching the man very carefully through the holes in the wall, stone-faced, speechless.

Then the man picked the girl up gently, held her on his shoulders and disappeared off in the street.

We swiftly left the area and headed home, silently, thoughtfully. The man's words still swept through my mind: "When love and mercy leave the world, then it is the beginning of the end."

BURREA'

The man in the dark uniform and balaclava flung the boy to the ground, violently.

"Get your hands on your head now."

Trembling uncontrollably and holding back tears of despair, the boy swallowed the impact of slamming against the marble floor, got up on his knees and placed his hands on his head, not daring to look up.

The second man by the doorway, also hidden beneath dark combat uniform and mask, produced a razor sharp army knife and gave it to his accomplice.

The boy glanced momentarily at the door which revealed the hallway and adjacent rooms of his home. The lifeless bodies of his mother and brothers, strewn on the floor, engulfed the view.

He looked down immediately, closed his eyes and waited. Nagging pain shot up from his liver. Blast. He cursed the heavens. He thought that of all the times his illness could have surfaced, it chose to appear right here, right now. Where was the justice?

The man who had barked the order moved up behind the boy, with the knife in his right hand.

He asked, rather nonchalantly: "What's your name, boy?"

The boy remained silent, obstinately facing the ground, shivering.

Suddenly, he felt a hard blow smack behind his right ear, which sent him crashing to the ground. The pain smothered him.

"I said tell me your name you stinking son of a whore! NOW!"

"Burrea'." He managed to whisper.

"What did you say, you little rat?"

"Burrea'."

"Burrea'?" The men looked at each other.

The one with the knife held the blade to boy's throat: "Listen here boy. Your fathers killed our children, your brothers raped our wives and mothers, and they invited our enemies into the land. Do you understand?"

Burrea' did not reply. The three people stood silently for a moment.

Then the other man spoke up: "Enough. Finish him and let's leave this pig sty."

Burrea' shivered as he felt the cold, clean blade tickle his neck. His traumatised tears rolled slowly down his eyes and fell upon the blade. Then, Burrea' felt something he had never felt before. It only took a few seconds and the transition was seamless, but the sensation rushed through him. The pain had disappeared. He opened his eyes and saw his own body crumpled on the floor below him but around him in the room, he noticed currents of light quivering and rocking to and fro. Burrea' smiled as the light flowed through him, holding him up like the hand of an angel.

The men marched out the house and both lit a cigarette and enjoyed a satisfying smoke. A darkness that they could not see grew around them, and just behind their necks, hidden in the air, voices whispered frantically, like a record playing forever: "May God curse you, may God curse you, may God curse you, may God curse you, may ..."

Notes:

Burrea': an Arabic word which means innocent.

This story is a personal attempt for me to come to terms with the terrible crimes which have been committed upon innocent women, children and people in Syria and also everywhere else where such crimes have been committed, like in Gazza, in Sierra Leone and other places.

May Allah spread His mercy upon the Syrian people and all the other innocents who have been murdered and may He inflict an almighty blow upon those who have committed these unforgivable crimes, ameen.

ARE YOU READY BROTHER?

The young man, clad in his combat uniform, sat up crossed-legged on his temporary bed, leaning back against the wall. He picked up a blue exercise book which lay by his side: his diary. The tip of an AK47 stuck out from under the bed and through the window opposite, a black flag, printed with the iconic stamp, flapped and shivered in the wind. The flag was wrapped around a metal pole which was attached to the white, bullet-ridden minaret of a burnt out mosque.

He looked at the first sentences that he had written on the page:

Why am I doing this? Well, there are several reasons.

He wiggled the black biro in his thumb and index finger and smiled inwardly. Then he continued:

Firstly, I'm doing it to please Allah the Almighty. Fighting for the cause of Allah is an obligation on every Muslim and Allah says that He will spread His bounty upon the one who is willing to give the Ultimate Sacrifice.

As he wrote this, a series of images and scenes flickered in his memory: him and his laptop, glowing in the night in his bed at home. The online conversations on the secret forum with "the brother": "Jihad is an obligation my brother and glad tidings to him who chooses Allah and jihad above all else." Then the speech, which was being shared on Wattsapp, by the famous sheikh, who was on the most-wanted list of the US government: "the infidels are causing mischief in our lands, will you just sit back?" The photographs on Facebook which had disturbed him the most, which had impelled him, which had filled him with such anger that he could not live with himself anymore, despite the fact that his medical career looked promising and his interview at the hospital had gone splendidly. Photos of the grotesque remains and charred body parts of children in the Middle-East flashed before him. Finally, he remembered his solitary readings of the Quran in the depths of the night, while his parents and siblings slept blissfully in their own bedrooms.

He continued writing: *I want to gain paradise and the holy station of shahadah; just like the great companions of Prophet Muhammad, peace be upon him. For this life is just a dream and the next life is a reality and striving for shahadah is the best preparation for that reality.*

He stopped and ran his fingers through his long dark wiry beard a few times, as was his wont when he was deep in thought. Another memory played itself like a short video clip in his head.

A week before leaving, he remembered that each night he picked up the Quran for guidance about the actions he was going to take. Sometimes he would close his eyes and randomly pick out a page and verse and look for an answer to his dilemmas. This was a practice that his mother used to do when she was in dire need. So he tried it also, as he hoped it would confirm the blessings in what he was about to embark upon.

But each night during that week, the verses he picked randomly all seemed to focus on two things: "And show kindness to your parents" and "Allah loves those who are the most conscious of Him." He remembered the disconcerting thoughts he felt that his random choices did not fall upon a verse on jihad and killing the disbelievers. He recollected the doubts that surfaced that week, as he sat alone in the darkness of his bedroom. Could this be a direct message from the divine to him? He read istikhara, the guidance prayer, every day that week, waiting for a sign, for a message, an indication. But nothing explicit manifested before him. Except for that the fact that every time he opened the holy book, it exhorted him to be kind to his parents and be aware of

God. Then the voice of "the brother" would chime in his head: "the devil will try to sow doubts in you before you leave, so be resolute. Shaytan hates it when one of Allah's servants prepares for jihad in the way of Allah".

As he sat there on the bed, pausing for a while, these memories played themselves out and he laughed to himself. Look at how the devil plays tricks on you. Even by using the holy book itself. More ideas began to flow and he busily wrote them down:

But another reason is that I'm taking a stand against the colonialism and reckless invasions of the USA and my own country, the UK. They speak of their civility, of their democracy, their human rights and their equality but they send their armed forces to bomb women and children in the Muslim world and they leave their puppet governments behind. I'm taking a stand against all this. If you see an evil, change it with your hand. That's exactly what I am doing, using the brain and the body that God has given me to make a change, in my own way, to this evil that is happening in the world. They have created a nightmare in our lands. They have attacked innocent civilians and left their countries in a state of civil war. That's why what I'm going to do will make them take a pause in their mischief-making. I am the spanner which will grind their works to a halt. Like Musa's stand before Pharaoh, my actions will shine the truth upon their falsehoods.

Suddenly, the face of his local imam appeared in his head and his Quranic commentary classes that he used to attend. Followed by the warm faces of his mother and father, then his childhood friends and family. He sighed:

The Muslims have lost their way. They no longer seek to fight in the cause of Allah and that is their disease. They lack the courage and the audacity to change things with their hands. I appreciate everything my family have done for me and I hope they understand why I am doing this. But sometimes, you have to put Allah before everyone and everything. And the Western governments and their agencies need to know that their assault on the Muslim world will not go unchallenged. If they bring fire, blood and anguish to us, we will bring fire, blood and anguish to them.

He paused. It felt like a great burden had been lifted from his heart. The voice of his school teacher surfaced: "writing can be therapeutic." This writing session seemed to have washed away any lingering doubts which were sticking to the walls of his conscience.

A knock rocked on the door.

"Come in," replied the young man, shutting his book and placing it to the side

A hulk of a man entered, uniformed, Middle-Eastern, crew-cut and great bushy beard.

"As salaamu alaykum! So, are you ready brother?" He asked after he shook the other's hand.

The young man smiled: "insha Allah. I am ready."

"Masha Allah, may Allah reward you! So remember, we will get you through the border again. We will drive you back to your hotel and you will catch your flight. Then we should hear the good news about your plane, tomorrow, insha Allah."

"Yes, of course, brother, insha Allah."

"Just make up a story if they ask you at the hotel where you have been. You can tell them you were staying with locals in the mountains. They will believe you. British people are doing it all the time."

"Insha Allah. Don't worry. I have the whole story in here," and he tapped his forehead with his forefinger.

"Okay, so be ready in the next hour. They will come to pick you up soon."

"Jazak Allah kheiran brother! Thanks for all your help."

"Insha Allah we will meet again in the next world," said the hulk as he embraced the young man who had risen to greet him.

"Insha Allah, the next world," replied the young man, glowing.

The man left the room and the younger one sat back on his bed and opened his diary again. He had a few more things he wanted to get off his chest so he grabbed the biro, lying on the bed next to him, and continued writing:

So, I am about to embark on a shorter journey which will lead onto a greater journey to another place, better than this one. May Allah accept my intentions and my actions. Truly, with Allah is the greatest success.

With that, he closed his diary, jumped up from his bed and began placing all his belongings into the grey backpack, which lay on his bed.

Subsequently, he tore off his combat uniform and wore the familiar garbs he had worn that night when they smuggled him into the camp: the jeans, the white t-shirt, the sunglasses and the clogs. He held the mobile phone which contained the hidden detonator and explosive. He was ready.

Suddenly, he heard a knock at the door. Time to go. He heaved his ruck-sack onto his shoulder and made for the door. But his gaze was riveted on the shelf before him. Upon it lay the Quran he had been reading. The one with the Arabic and the English.

He hesitated and just stared at it for a while. Some kind of force deep within impelled him to pick it up. He tried to resist but it was too much for him. He thought to himself: *if I encounter something that fills me with doubt, it is from the devil. If it offers me encouragement, it is from Allah.* In a flash, he swept up the holy book and opened it to a random page and line. He read the verse and found that his heart seemed to rise and fall like a yoyo dangling inside a pit of darkness:

"We ordained for the Children of Israel that if anyone slew a person - unless it be in retaliation for murder or for spreading mischief in the land - it would be as if he slew all mankind: and if anyone saved a life, it would be as if he saved the life of all humanity."

He knew this verse well because the local imam back home, Qaari Saab, had presented its meaning to him during that time when he had been under the influence of "moderate" Muslims or as he called them now, the "house Muslims":

"This is first and foremost a rule for the Children of Israel, so not a direct command to Muslims," Qaari Saab had said during one of their classes, "to kill in retaliation or for spreading mischief is effectively war instituted by the state, capital punishment and an instrument of the government- not an excuse to take the law into your own hands. To kill any innocent person is as bad as killing the whole of humanity." Qaari Saab's sober voice echoed in his head.

Innocent people…Sowing mischief… He thought about all the people who would die after he detonated the bomb and himself in the aeroplane in less than twenty-four hours. Qaari Saab's words filled his head again: "it is only lawful to kill someone if you are in authority and have gone through due process. This is what the verse suggests, otherwise, you have committed mass slaughter."

Then the voice of "the brother" shook inside his head. For he had also interpreted the verse for him online: "it means it is lawful to kill these people and yourself because each tax paying kaafir has voted for a government which is spreading mischief in our lands. Male or female, old or young, Muslim or non-Muslims. You are giving your life because there is no other effective way of creating such a loss to the enemy."

The two voices chimed in his mind, competing for a hold over him:

"It is as if you have killed the whole of mankind…"

"They are your enemy; they are not innocent…"

The young man stood there gazing at that verse in the Quran that he held in his hands, transfixed. He could not move.

A barrage of knocking woke him from his trance:

A voice yelled: "are you ready brother?"

LAW AND LOVE

"We have three reliable witnesses," explained Mullah Ameer, "who are ready to testify that Azmat Khan consumed whisky and consorted with an unknown courtesan during his nephew's wedding." And with that, he gazed across the bare room, where Mullah Ghazi sat against the wall, resting against a cushion. The latter looked worried, like his heart was aching.

"So, he will face the judges and he will feel the penalty. This district will see how serious we are; they will see the law of Allah ruling over them."

After some silence, Mullah Ghazi looked up at Mullah Ameer and sighed. His large, deep eyes swelled with remorse:

"You know that he is sorry and you know that this has not become public knowledge yet."

Mullah Ameer sat up from his divan, which he had been resting against, "what are you saying Ghazi Khan?"

"I am saying that the man has repented, his sin is a secret and he is not proud of what he has done."

Mullah Ameer's voice hardened, "how can you be so sure?"

"Because he came to see me personally; he shed tears, he knows it was a mistake."

"So you think this is good enough."

"Do you think what he has done for us is good enough?"

Mullah Ameer shook with anger: "don't speak to me like this Ghazi Khan. I know Azmat Khan's generosity to the poor is without comparison, but why have you become so soft all of a sudden? Even Nabi Mohammad peace be upon him said if his own daughter were to steal then he would be the first to present her hands. The justice of Allah is swift... and it will be better for him to serve his punishment here…Why am I even telling you this? You know all of this yourself." He stopped and regarded Ghazi Khan, who had stood and listened to him with a mournful look in his eye.

"Ghazi Khan, spit it out. What troubles you?"

Mullah Ameer noticed that tears shimmered and glistened in Ghazi's eyes. And for the first time for many years, Ameer, who had seen Ghazi fight off a whole troop of occupying soldiers single-handedly, felt like his old friend was suddenly losing his resolution, like a withering flame.

"I had a dream and I saw a vision."

Mullah Ameer laughed out briefly: "You saw a dream…And what did you see?" Incredulity was creeping into his voice.

Ghazi Khan spoke vividly: "I saw Nabi Mohammad, Allah bless him and grant him; I saw him as clearly as the full moon in the clear night sky. His beauty took my breath away. I have not stopped weeping ever since. And there was a look in his eye…It penetrated my core, so much, and that I saw something which makes me cry even more."

Unimpressed, Ameer responded: "And what was that?"

"I saw my ignorance and I saw the hardness of my heart…" Suddenly Ghazi's haunted expression transformed into an undeniable intensity: "My brother, the sharia is the very reason that I breathe, but let me tell you clearly, you are wrong to pursue this case. For I have learned that mercy is the fountain from which our Prophet drinks. And you show no mercy by punishing Azmat Khan," Ghazi stopped momentarily, noticing Ameer's growing fury clouding over his face, but he was unperturbed: "and it does not stop with Azmat Khan…We have no right to wield the sword of justice unless we have been fully drenched in Mustafa's bottomless ocean of mercy."

Ameer could not hold himself back: "Ghazi Khan! Stop blabbering like a two penny dervish and come back to reality!"

"No, Ameer Khan, you look at what is within you and look into the heart of the Prophet, then evaluate what we really are."

Suddenly, Ameer unsheathed his bowie knife: "you have become a deviant Ghazi Khan and you must be stopped!"

In a flash, Ghazi Khan unleashed his own razor sharp dagger and cried: "I am for you!"

The two men were suddenly flanked either side, by their men, who rushed in looking concerned, with their revolvers ready.

Ghazi Khan and Ameer Khan glared at each other for a while but then lowered their weapons.

"I only want the law of Allah to reign supreme in our land," stated Mullah Ameer calmly now, smothering his rage.

"And I only want Allah's truth and mercy to prevail," replied Ghazi Khan, unshaken.

And with that, the two groups of men, crowned with pristine, black turbans and flowing salwar kameez, stood perfectly still.

WHEN BILLY SMITH MET
THE MULLAHS

"I just want to love God, I blurted out...."
Piscine: *The Life of Pi*

Billy Smith was a quiet little English boy who lived on a working class estate in Bradford. Although he was only twelve, Billy had an extremely deep approach to life, unlike all the other kids. His mum noticed this even when he was a baby. Laughing and giggling at things she could not see or comprehend, his mum thought that her son seemed to exist on a heavenly plain. And what a difference between Billy and the typical lads around him when he grew older! While he would sit in awe, watching the splendour of the setting sun or marvel at the starlings looping in the grey sky, the other kids would point at him and laugh. They just played Xbox.

But Billy's contemplation became so deep, that he made an unprecedented step in his family's history. A step which mildly perplexed his mum; which shocked his granny so much that she spat out her false teeth and prompted some of his teachers to suggest counselling. Yes, he had converted to Islam.

How he became a Muslim was a simple yet profound story. But what he said one day to the two mullahs became the stuff of local Islamic legend.

It was on a Friday, when Billy got a little bit lost on the way back from school and he passed by two mosques on the same road. It was here that his journey to Islam began rather dramatically.

At the top there was a converted office building, topped with a modest little green dome, which was now called Masjid Abu Bakr. And down the bottom there was a grand, purpose-built mosque like something out of a Mughal history book. Below its lustrous green dome the grand sign read: Masjid Ghausia.

However, it was two things, two words, in fact, which took Billy's breath away that day. First he noticed the word, Allah, in gold Arabic letters cresting the doorway of Abu

Bakr Masjid. Billy noticed the shape of the word, the letters: A L L A H. And then, he was lost... Lost to himself, the world and everything else. He was lost in love... Love for that word, whatever it said.

A Muslim devotee stepped out of the doorway. Billy asked him:

"What does that say above the doorway?"

The Muslim looked and smiled: "It says Allah. Allah is the name of God in our religion." And he walked away.

Billy walked on, mesmerised. That feeling of love was engulfing him. It was immense. He felt like he was going to explode, not physically, but inside, in his spirit. Not just for the word, but for the One who the name represented. God, Allah. Whoever that was.

He felt like he just about to crumple on the floor in a flood of tears, when he found himself staring at something outside the gates of the Ghausia masjid. Another word, in that strange language. Was it Urdu? Arabic? Pakistani? Billy didn't have a clue. But what he did notice was equally sensational. When he looked at this word, which was etched onto a gold plate on the right side of the main entrance, he felt a wonderful sweetness and calmness. The intensity of love that he felt ebbed and settled so that he didn't feel like exploding any more.

A Muslim walked out of the door, crowned with a wonderful green turban. To Billy, the man looked like he had just walked out of a film set from Sinbad the Sailor.

The Muslim smiled broadly at Billy. Billy also asked him:

"What does that say next to the door?"

After glancing at the word, the Muslim smiled again: "It says Muhammad, Ya Muhammad. And on the other side it says Ya Allah. Allah is the name of our God. Muhammad is the name of our Prophet."

Billy thought for a moment about the way he was feeling and said:

"Excuse me, but have you got a leaflet which has those two words on there. I've got some homework to do." Good thinking. That would make his interest sound more plausible.

"Sure!" And the green turbaned man walked back into the mosque and returned with a little leaflet which said: An Introduction to Islam.

And right there, at the top of the leaflet, Billy could see the two words which had arrested his heart and made him feel a way he had never felt before. Allah, the name of God. And Muhammad the name of God's prophet.

He took the leaflet home. His mum was too busy to notice what was going on. But deep within, Billy was experiencing a rapid transformation. He felt like a grubby little caterpillar growing wings and being filled up with colour. With the colours of love. Not lust. He had learned about puberty at school. It wasn't that. It was something different. This love made him feel so great that he wanted to cry forever. And every time he looked at the name, Allah, on the leaflet, he felt suddenly overcome, like he was being drowned in light. He couldn't handle it. But then all he had to do was to look at the name Muhammad, and this calmed him down and gave him some relief.

He loved this new feeling and he wanted to find out more about it. So he decided that he would make a visit to the two mosques he had passed. Masjid Abu Bakr and Masjid Ghausia.

This is where things got little bit more interesting, or should we say explosive...

So two weeks had elapsed, Billy read the leaflet carefully, learning the information comprehensively, then soon enough, he became well-known to both mosques. However, he kept two things a secret. One: why he came to Islam. Two: he hid the fact that he attended both mosques, from his mother and from the two opposing congregations.

The first thing he did when he visited both mosques was to announce to the youngsters there, that he had come to Islam of his own accord and had proclaimed the shahadah in another mosque in Bradford. Neither mosque therefore could credit themselves with his conversion. But it was Billy's style that made him loved.

In the Abu Bakr mosque, after introducing himself he said: "I want to know about Allah, tell my about Allah. For I love to see his name."

The brothers at Abu Bakr mosque responded heartily:

"What an abid!"

"What a Momin!"

"What a gora!"

When he went to the Ghausia mosque, the youngsters there exulted as they heard him say: "Muhammad, tell me about Muhammad, for I love to see his name."

"What an ashiq!"

"What a lover!"

"What a gora!"

But what he kept a secret was that in Abu Bakr mosque, he felt the love for Allah surge through his veins and lift him up into a sky of lustrous light. Light filled with endless love. So at Abu Bakr mosque he would do his maghrib.

His astral projections at the Abu Bakr mosque would leave him dizzy and on the verge of a breaking point, so he would pray his Isha at the Ghausia mosque. There, the pain and ecstasy left him and the soothing name of Muhammad, peace be upon him, calmed the stormy seas within his heart.

So his simultaneous attendance of each mosque remained a secret, until one day... After he had been absent due to illness, two rather striking characters turned up outside his door.

That day, his mother was interrupted from her knitting by two separate loud knocks on her front door. It was midday, just after Zohr prayers at the mosques. Billy had just finished his prayer and lay resting in bed. The sick note from his doctor lay neatly by his side for comfort. School wasn't one of Billy's favourite places.

Anyway, the two loud separate knocks echoed through the house and mum reacted with:

"Cor blimey! Someone's in a hurry!" And mum made her way to the front door.

She wrenched opened the front door and was just about to tell off the hooligans who had so rudely disturbed her sewing, when she noticed the two personalities standing there.

On one side, a bearded gentleman, Asian-looking, wearing a long white robe, a white turban, a bit like Usama Bin Laden, mum thought to herself. And on the other side, another Muslim, same beard, they almost looked like twins. Only this one wore a long white tunic and baggy trousers, and his turban was as orange as mum's jar of marmalade.

Both of them stood, aware of each other's presence, with an air of discomfort.

"Oh! How can I...er...help you gentlemen?" Mum was kind of lost for words.

"Hello, Missus, my name is Ghulam Rasul, I come from the mosque down the road, *Ghausia*." And as he mentioned, *Ghausia* he straightened his back and shifted his orange turban a little.

"Yes, hello, missus, I'm Abdul Ahad, I'm from the Mosque, further down the road, *Abu Bakr*." And he pronounced *Abu Bakr* in a very clear manner, enunciating each syllable very clearly, as if he was making a really point of it.

There was an awkward silence. Mum didn't have a clue what they were talking about.

"Okay, thanks for that...But how can I help you?" Mum was growing rather tired of these two.

"It's about your son…" begun Ghulam.

"I wanted to see how he was doing," interrupted Abdul Ahad.

"Because he hasn't attended mosque for a while, so I just wanted to check," interjected Ghulam.

"If he is okay," added Abdul.

The two glanced at each other, uncomfortably, then looked at mum.

"Okay, you want to see Billy." Mum was very polite and didn't hold a trace of racism in her heart, but she was rather perturbed to see these Muslim-types interested in her son. She wanted to know what was going on. "Alright, you better come in then."

"What both of us?" Ghulam began.

"Me, with him?" Asked Abdul, pointing at the man opposite.

Bemused, Mum replied: "Ye-ees, the two of you, if that's okay? Come this way."

Neither of them could hide their annoyance and they simultaneously walked into the offered open door. A second later, mum looked back to find both men wedged in the doorway, and then with an almighty push, they stumbled forward into Billy's house, nearly knocking over mum's decoration pieces in the landing.

"Oh so sorry," said Ghulam, while glaring at his adversary.

"Likewise." Replied Abdul equally bitter.

"Please gentlemen, come this way, Billy's in here."

They walked into the living room where mother announced their arrival and Billy, having realised what had happened here, began shrinking underneath his quilt while he lay on the sofa. He had met both of these characters before; they always gave him a lecture every time he visited the mosques; he didn't really like them. In fact, the average worshippers at each mosque labelled them the "wannabe mullahs!"

"Hi Billy, I've got some visitors for you, some well-wishers, the Muslims from down the road!"

Ghulam took a seat to the right and Abdul made sure he was safely to the left.

Once again, the awkward silence hovered over the four of them.

"I'll get a cup of tea then," offered mum, breaking the silence and disappearing into the kitchen. What they didn't know was that mum was hiding behind the corner, listening in to the following conversation whilst making the tea in the kitchen.

Billy looked at both men in dismay and realised he would have to explain himself.

"So Billy."

"Brother Billy."

"Ashiq Billy."

"Tablighi Billy!"

"I have come to see how you are doing and to ask if you need any help from us at Abu Bakr mosque," said Abdul, taking the lead.

"Yes, but of course, you will come for help at Al Ghausia first won't you?" Retorted Ghulam.

Billy didn't know what to say.

"Billy, I didn't realise that…"

"You went to …"

"*Their* mosque," and both men pointed at each other as they announced this discomforting fact. For a moment, their index fingers remained pointing sideways in each other's directions, kind of hovering in mid-air, then after noticing they promptly put them down.

"Yes, I do like going to Abu Bakr Mosque and to Ghausia Mosque."

Ghulam Rasul laughed and then became serious: "Now brother Billy, that is all well and good, but I must advise you sincerely that you should avoid attending *that* mosque."

Abdul Ahad coughed loudly and added: "Well actually akhi, I would advise you to avoid this mosque, *Ghausia.*" And he gave some sarcastic emphasis to the final word.

"Erm… I don't see what the problem is with…" Billy's explanation was quickly interrupted.

"Brother Billy, you don't understand, I am only saying this to protect your aquida," began Ghulam.

"And I am only telling you to protect you from innovation," replied Abdul.

Ghulam's voice was now steadily rising: "You must be protected from, well, how can I put it? Munafiqs!"

Abdul wasn't having any of it and matched Ghulam's intensity: "I have to warn you until it's too late, until you fall into bida and shirk!"

Ghulam's turban shook: "Billy, they are gustakei Rasul!"

Abdul waved his fingers at Ghulam: "Billy! They are biddatees!"

"They denigrate our Prophet!"

"They worship our Prophet!"

"They will take you away for forty days to Pakistan!"

"They will make you sing to Madina all day and make you miss your prayers!"

"How dare you! Gustakh!"

"Take a hike, bidatee!"

"Acha! Fir bihar ar jow, mei aap ko teek karown ga!"

"Fine let's step outside, Mr Bida Shirk!"

Suddenly mum appeared in the room: "Now gentlemen, I think we need to calm down..."

Ghulam jumped up from the sofa and said with passion: "No, missus! This is challenge between truth and falsehood!"

"Now you will see the haqq vanquish the batil!" Announced Abdul, rising.

Then Billy couldn't take it anymore and jumped off the sofa: "I JUST WANT TO LOVE ALLAH AND HIS PROPHET!" He yelled.

Abdul fell silent and straightened his robe. Ghulam held on to his turban as if it was going to fall off, and mum said: "Billy? I didn't know you'd become....Muslim?"

Billy looked down, tears beginning to flood his eyes. "Mum, I was going to tell you, and I was waiting for the right time. Yes I follow Islam, and I love Allah and Prophet Muhammad, I've never felt this way before about anything. It fills me with love and light."

Mum was awestruck: "okay dear, I only want what's best for you."

"And you two," at that, both mullahs coughed a little in embarrassment: "I love both of your mosques. I love the way you talk about Allah at Abu Bakr mosque, and I love the passion and the songs about Prophet Muhammad at Ghausia mosque. Can't I just attend both mosques?"

"Yes, erm… Can't he attend both churches...I mean mosques?" Added Mum, trying be a help.

"Well, er, you know..." Began Ghulam.

"It's like this, it's er, not really that...." Attempted Abdul.

Suddenly, they both said in unison: "Brother Billy, good luck!" And with that, they promptly left the room. However, they both got wedged in the doorway again and mum had to do a run up and give them a little push to set them on their ways. Then Abdul Ahad strode away to Abu Bakr mosque and Ghulam Rasul marched off, humming the latest Owais Qadri track.

"Right son, now it's time you came clean." And mum sat with her son and heard the story of the how Billy had become mesmerised by the word Allah and the word Muhammad, peace be upon him. The story actually brought a smile mum's face and all she could say was this:

"Look son. As long as all this doesn't disturb your education, or take you away from me, you have my blessing." Mother and son then embraced and smiled.

In the following days, Billy found that Abdul Ahad, Ghulam Rasul and their cliques paid little more interest to Billy. In their eyes, he was just a confused Gora who didn't fit in. But he managed to strike a lasting relationship with the two gentlemen he had met the first time he saw the name of God, Allah and the name of His Prophet, Muhammad, peace be upon. The man with the green turban at Ghausia mosque was called Aashiq Ali, and the man from Abu Bakr was called Owais. When he asked both men about why they prayed in their respective mosques and didn't really mix, amazingly, they gave him the same answer, and then didn't talk about the issue again. Instead they preferred to say their prayers and offer their own unique acts of worship and praise. Aashiq Ali loved to sing naats and send prayers and blessings upon the Prophet, and Owais loved to spend his time pondering on the meanings of the Quran. Billy found solace in both of their expressions of love for Allah and for Allah's Prophet.

But what they said to him would stay etched in his heart, as he grew and matured in the love that he had found for Allah and for Prophet Muhammad, peace be upon him:

"Allah's beauty shines upon us and we love to stay in those places where we feel it the most."

THE KNIGHTS OF LOVE AND CAUTION

Two knights stood face to face, engaged in ferocious combat, with swords swirling and crashing against each other, like the rough seas pounding the rocky cliffs.

Suddenly they were surrounded by the king's men, hundreds of armed guards. Razor-sharp arrowheads were pointing at the knights from all directions, ready to launch.

A guard in ceremonial garb stepped forward and announced:

"Drop your swords and return for immediate appointment with his majesty the king!"

The knights surrendered their arms and followed the guards back through the forest path and up the hills, where the royal castle stood in magnificence and glory.

It wasn't long before both knights, still clad in their armour, stood before their wondrous king and master, who was seated magnificently upon his throne, which had roots that grew out of the centre of the earth. By his side, stood his royal highness, the prince. A young man of the most exquisite beauty, flawless intellect and divine temperament.

"Well," began the king, imperiously, looking down upon both of his knights, "explain this regrettable conflict to me."

The first knight began: "Sire, my fellow's love for your prince has gone to such an extent, in my eyes, that he promotes him over you. Indeed there was some news that your prince sought to usurp you. And, subsequently, I confronted his royal highness, rather roughly I might add. I only had your security in mind, my lord. But my adversary here, who was once a friend, felt I had committed an unforgivable crime and attacked me. The way I see it, he has failed in his duty as a knight and his love for our prince has become an obsession. This love has eclipsed his duty to your security. When he attacked me, I was but defending myself." And with that, he knelt down on one knee and finished with: "my Lord, I did it for you."

The King sat, unmoved, and cast his gaze upon the second knight.

"And you, explain the meaning of this sorry affair."

"Well, dear sire, I heard of the antics of my erstwhile friend, and his rough treatment of your beloved son, his royal highness the prince. And I could not withhold my rage at such impertinence. I felt I had to punish the prince's oppressor. So I fought him. To restore the honour of your son. In my view, he is no longer a knight. How can he be if he has no remorse about abusing the ones he is supposed to protect? How can he mistreat such a paragon like our prince! I attacked him and I had only had my love for you and for your prince as my motivation."

And with that, he knelt and then stood back.

The king sat there, a smile spreading upon his face, which was quickly replaced with a perfect image of indisputable authority. He beckoned one of the knights to approach his seat.

"As for you," he said, gazing at the first knight. "Your intention was to protect me from a possible threat, even from my own son, I commend you for that. But engrossed in your sense of duty and fervour, you ignored my statutes, that abuse of any form of my prince carries a death sentence. For you know that I love my prince more than anything above and below the sun, the skies and the seas. I know the prince better than anyone of you; I know the very thoughts in his soul! You know little of how great he is. I know you love me and you were loyal to me, but you harmed the thing that I love the best in your belief that you were defending me. You broke my statute. How could you not recognize that your counterpart was in the throes of love! How could you use such language about my one and only prince! Your obsession with caution blinded you to the reality of my love, the secret of which dwells in my love for my prince. So, I have made my judgement and shall carry it out in time. You may retire."

The first knight stood back.

The king beckoned the second knight towards him.

"And as for you. You acted out of love for me and for my prince. You felt my honour and the honour of my beloved prince had been attacked, so you raised your sword in my defence and the defence of my statutes. You remembered that a swift punishment befalls the one who tries to harm my prince. And I commend you for that. But in your raging love for my prince, you forgot the principle of caution and restraint. For many a king has been usurped by his own son. And many a knight has been the instigator of such rebellions. You loved me and my prince truly. But in the throes of your love, you forgot that dangers can emerge if once neglects caution. You attacked one of my knights, though you had a reason. But I cannot have my knights fighting in public. It creates the wrong impression. It may lead our enemies to think we are weak and use this dispute to spread disunity and conflict amongst us. So I have considered a judgement and shall carry it out in time. You may retire."

Both knights stood back, facing the ground with perfect humility.

The king arose and left his royal throne, closely followed by his beloved son, both retiring for the royal supper.

The courtiers and guards, in their hundreds, encircling the two knights began whispering. Half siding with the caution of the first knight and the other half touched by the love of the second knight.

Their story spread through the lands, far and wide, and raging debates sparked off in all corners of the kingdom about which knight was right and which was wrong. The two knights became famously known as the Knights of Love and Caution.

AYYAN KIRSHI WALI AND THE MAJDHOOB

One night, after a sell-out conference, entitled: "Female, Apostate and Proud", Ayyaan Kirshi Wali strolled towards her car in the car park outside the convention centre, when her attention was drawn by a most singular woman.

She looked African, like herself, East-African to be exact. Lean, slender, swan-like neck and chin. A veritable East-African princess! But she was shrouded in a long, drab robe and her dark headscarf kept slipping around revealing exquisite curls and locks. What a beauty!

However, this woman was in a state of total turmoil, heaving, wailing, crying out, shaking her head to and fro.

"He's thrown me out! He's thrown me out!" She cried.

Ayyaan rushed towards this poor woman, her heart melting and her conscience informing her that this was a lost sheep who needed the Kirshi Wali form of guidance.

"He's thrown me out! He's thrown me out." The tragic woman cried again "where will I go? What will I do?"

Tears streamed from this woman like a brook flowing through a diamond mine.

Ayyaan took hold of her fellow woman, clasped her onto her shoulder and allowed her to sob her heart out.

"Don't worry my dear," reassured Ayyaan, "it's all going to be alright."

The woman just sobbed and her muffled voice could be heard from Ayyan's shoulder:

"No, no. It's all gone to ruin. Without him life is not worth living for a second. He's thrown me out over nothing!"

Ayyaan listened and thought it sounded like a familiar story, so her voice slightly hardened out of a pious indignation at this woman's plight.

"What did you do? I suppose you were guilty of just looking at someone else..."

"Yes, yes!" The woman exclaimed, "My glance fell on others just momentarily and now he's thrown me out!"

Ayyaan pressed on- she wanted to know everything.

"Did your father make you go with him?"

"My father taught me how to be with him," she cried, "but now I have been thrown out due to a loss of manners."

"Did he and your father, make you, you know..." Ayyaan looked at her, knowingly.

"Yes, yes! He wanted me to mutilate myself so I mutilated myself the way he wanted me to, until he was satisfied to accept me into his presence."

Anger rose from Ayyaan's voice: "typical, typical of these brutes and their brutish ways and their brutish cult, all designed to punish us!"

Between tears, the woman answered, "Although it sounds oppressive, I cannot survive without him, I really can't!

"Sister," Ayyaan exclaimed passionately, "Forget him! Think for yourself. Free yourself from the shackles of these men and their structures and become a freethinker. A free woman. A free mind." Ayyaan's voice rang with a righteous tune of authority and confidence.

The woman stopped sobbing, bowed her head, closed her eyes and just stood there, as if in a trance.

Ayyaan stood back, perplexed.

"Madam, are you okay?"

The woman remained standing, still as a statue, the wind swirling and curling gently around them. The moon shone in the night sky; a heavenly lamp.

Then she looked up at Ayyaan and what was astonishing was that her face had turned from anguish to utter ecstasy. Those eyes shone with a beauty that seemed timeless. The light literally poured out.

Ayyaan regarded her, at first perplexed, but then she felt a growing bewilderment creeping into her settled notions of reality.

"He has invited me back in now. Jazak Allah kheiran!"

And with a final gleaming smile that would melt the heart of a gladiator, the strange woman disappeared into the night.

Ayyaan walked back to her car, with an uncomfortable intimation whispering in her heart.

All she could hear was a voice that kept saying: "free yourself of those shackles...."

Notes:

Majdhoob: a spiritual aspirant whose love for God has made him or her deranged. In the Muslim world, these people can be venerated and held in esteem.

THE TICKET

Adam suddenly caught glance of it on his windscreen and felt his blood boil like a bubbling volcano. That white slip stuck there like a clumsy plaster on his car. A penalty ticket.

"Oi!" He shouted after the uniformed man, casually strolling ahead. The man promptly swivelled around.

"What the hell do you call this?" Adam roared, pointing at the ticket on the windscreen of his people-carrier. "I was only ten minutes over my parking time, I just literally popped in the library to return some books. HOW CAN YOU BE SO TIGHT?"

The traffic warden, covered in green official wear, foreign-looking, Asian perhaps, stepped up to Adam, with a smile on his face.

Adam changed his tack.

"Brother, come on. I bought a ticket. I wasn't taking the mick. I was just over by ten minutes. Only ten minutes. Come on brother, give me a break. "

With an impish smile, the traffic warden could only answer: "sorry."

"Sorry? What do you mean?"

"Sorry." Replied the warden, smirking.

"Sorry...Is that all you can say. Sorry?" Rage began to flood through Adam's arteries. "I PAID FOR A TICKET. I TOOK THE TROUBLE TO PAY FOR A BLASTED TICKET AND NOW YOU EXPECT ME TO PAY ANOTHER GODFORSAKEN THIRTY QUID FOR BEING TEN MINUTES LATE WHEN I HAD ALREADY BOUGHT A TICKET. WHAT THE HELL DO YOU TAKE ME FOR?"

Adam moved closer to the man, barking in his face. The traffic warden closed his eyes and let the storm blow through him. Passers-by stopped and gawked. Some smiled sympathetically; others frowned.

"YOU ARE A SCUMBAG. FILTHY ROTTEN SCUMBAG. YOU JUST WANT ANOTHER VICTIM FOR YOUR FILTHY ROTTEN COMMISSION SUCKING BOSSES WHO'VE PROMISED YOU A HAPPY MEAL IF YOU REACH YOUR DAILY TARGET YOU FILTHY ROTTEN SCUMBAG!!!"

The traffic warden wiped off the drizzle of spit from his nose and cheeks. Adam, seething like an American wrestler, waited for his response. For Adam, the world had turned various shades of red and he suddenly remembered that this same phenomenon had occurred earlier this week when he let rip on his wife and last week, when he got out of his car and swore at the driver who had been tailgating him on the high road.

"Sorry." The traffic warden spoke at last. Crazy smile again. Adam sighed in despair and the traffic warden disappeared down the road.

Adam took a deep breath, gathered himself and then blushed. For his public audience dotted around the road held their gazes on him.

"Sorry..." He announced to them and peeled off the ticket from his windscreen.

He began to read it, but the whole ticket was blank, except for some words, which he read:

LAA TAGHDAB

LAA TAGHDAB

LAA TAGHDAB

An ear-splitting ring rattled all around. Adam winced and covered his ears. He opened his eyes, found himself in his bedroom, arose from his bed and slammed on the mute button of the clock radio.

Fajr time...

His wife arose quickly, nervous of what might come next, meekly asking: "is everything okay?"

Adam looked ahead, his eyes welling up. Those words on the ticket, melting his soul.

"Sorry..."

NOTES:

LAA TAGHDAB: Arabic words- don't be angry. These are the famous words of the Prophet Muhammad, upon him and his family be peace and blessings, when he gave advice to one of his companions, emphasising the sentence many times. Many Muslims understand this to show the importance of avoiding blameworthy anger in one's life.

SUFI WILAYAT

Wilayat, or should I say, Sufi Wilayat, looked down at his zikr counter, which read, one thousand. This made him smile. "Masha Allah! Alhamdulillah!" He proudly pronounced, thinking to himself that later on today he was going to push himself to do another thousand duroode paak. He then arose from his prayer mat that he had bought from his last umrah trip and headed downstairs, where his wife of thirty years, Rasheeda, was preparing his typical breakfast: Pakistani tea, a rich paratha with scrambled eggs, and "Priya's Good Morning Show" on the GEO channel in the background.

His name was Wilayat Khan, but now, in his mature age, he liked to be called Sufi Wilayat, especially as for the last few years he had begun living the life of a pious Muslim and frequenting the gatherings of prominent Sufi sheikhs in the UK. He particularly enjoyed hearing his wife referring to him as Sufi Saab when she was talking about him to other people. However, nobody ever heard the other names she often labelled him within the safe boundaries of their home, when she felt slightly miffed by his laziness and inability to place his socks in the washing basket.

Sufi Wilayat had much more time on his hands these days, since he had retired and all his kids were at university. He could now attend Friday prayers, and even Eid prayers were no longer a problem. He would sigh when he thought about all the prayers he had missed, but then the idea would arise that Allah, the Almighty, is ever-forgiving! And more to the point, Allah would understand that he had put in all those extra shifts in the taxi rank because he had to build that plaza and villa back in Mirpur and he did have to sign on for all those years because one day his children would need the money when they go to university to be doctors and also when they got married to his nephews and nieces back home. He smiled to think that one day his beautiful niece, Ruksheeda, would be gracing his house with her beautiful cooking and hard work. And no more terrible scalding from Rasheeda! But then another unpalatable reality surfaced in his head, that his eldest son, Mustafa, whose was betrothed to Ruksheeda, had recently come home talking about a pious, Moroccan girl he had met at university, which Wilayat quickly buried into his subconscious, before going downstairs to his long suffering wife, Rasheeda.

A sizzling, heavenly plate of paratha and egg, with steaming dood-patti greeted him as he sat down in the living room, and as Priya, a "modrun" looking Pakistani female presenter, with her immaculately straightened hair and cheela flying around her neck like a hoop, was having some great guftagoo with some famous vocal artist from Lahore with a hair transplant.

Sufi Wilayat chomped away. Rasheeda sat, smiling at Priya and studying her dupatta, the print on her salwar qameez and the way she was flicking her hair back and forth.

Sufi Saab finished his breakfast with a satisfying fog horn of a belch and slurped up on his tea, before grabbing his coat and going for his daily walk.

Rasheeda's eyes were still fastened to Priya. The singer from Lahore was giving some acapella renditions to which Priya was clapping, while her dupatta was flapping about her neck.

"Have you done your wird?" Wilayat asked Rasheeda, just as he was leaving.

Rasheeda ignored him because she was engrossed in the show.

"I said, have you done your wird yet? Can't you hear me?"

Finally she looked up, irritated: "I'll do it, I'll do it."

Wilayat looked at her disapprovingly: "Don't say I'll do it. Do it now! What's more important, your Rabb or Priya! I did my wird and I also finished one thousand durood, masha Allah. Don't waste your time!"

Rasheeda gave him one of those scornful looks and then replied: "where are you going today?"

Hurt by her comeback Wilayat shouted: "You know where I'm going! For my daily walk up town!"

"Well don't forget the Jang this time, and make sure you lock the door properly."

Sufi Wilayat quickly disappeared, locked the door carefully and then walked into the cold, autumn morning, down his road and up towards town.

A talk from one of the local pirs was chiming in his mind.

"Some of the Sufis reached their greatest openings because they had to show patience with their wives and family, especially as they did lots of zikr on their own. And the openings happened, without warning, where they least expected it..."

Sufi Saab thought of this and smiled. Today could be the day. He had been hurt by his wife and deeply troubled by his son. Could this be the day when Allah sent him into the plains of fana and baqa? Could this be the moment when all the zikr and prayers he had been doing since he reached the age of fifty-two was rewarded by the almighty? Could this be the day that he became, like, a pir...? With light shining around his face. Disciples flocking from everywhere. His own TV channel. His own centre in Mirpur. Could this be the day?

He slipped out of his stupor because a taxi driver was shouting at him: "well go on then! It's green!"

Wilayat looked up and realised the green man was flashing and he should quickly cross the road before the gawking drivers ran him over.

He kept walking. The stories of the great saints, flowing around his mind. The fact that he had done one thousand duroodei paak. This could be the day. He decided to put his will in the hand of Allah and just, walk...Without direction. Just walk and see where the winds of divine love took him. And he walked and walked. After a while, he felt like he was floating; like he had arisen. He felt like he was on a heavenly plain. He entered a building, taking no notice of where he was. This could be the moment. Imagine it! His opening was going to happen in the middle of the town centre! He could feel it. The saints in the barzakh would appear before his eyes. He would hear the beating of a sparrow's heart, twittering away in the forests beyond. He could see the mureeds, crowding around to see the light shining off his face.

He entered a room. He stopped. Closed his eyes and waited. Suddenly, he felt himself rising off the ground and ascending into the sky. This could be his own, special miraaj! This could be his moment of receiving the faiz from his sheikh. This could be... Then he waited, expectant, ready for his lord to bring him near, when he heard an unmistakeable voice announcing clear as day:

"Level 3. Men's Underwear and Socks. Thank you for shopping at Marks and Spencers".

THE SOLDIER

"You're home and dry," whispered the Devil.

A nervous, young soldier, waited impatiently in the depths of his trench. Listening carefully, he held his breath. For a whole minute he heard silence ruling above him and it seemed that the bullets and bombs had stopped. Hope rising in his heart and feeling the strain of this long, hard, protracted war, he was sure this was a telling sign. Inwardly, he wrestled with his conscience. Fear stated that he should remain cautious and in a state of ever present alertness. Hope said, this was just rewards for his long hard slog, for holding the fort, for his indefatigability. Fear, hope. Hope, fear. Fear, hope. Hope, fear. Oscillating for a while, he sat against the mud and the stench of his trench, becoming increasingly exasperated. He gripped his rifle tightly, clenched his teeth, closed his eyes, then looked up at the sky for help. The silence and peace was just irresistible. Fear, hope. Hope fear. Fear, hope. Hope, fear. Hope. That was it. Resolute, he thought it was now safe to chance it above.

Out in the open, he witnessed the clear, open battlefield in complete silence and stillness, as if time had stopped. Thinking the coast was clear, he advanced, his rifle at the ready, his wits about him.

He walked several steps now, thinking he had reached freedom and victory. He even started dreaming of his arrival home to his neighbourhood where he would be hailed a hero and carried on the backs of his friends and doted on by the pretty girls.

Suddenly he snapped out of his daydream and found that he had reached the trench of the enemy. He looked below carefully to find it was empty. The enemy seemed to have retreated. What joy! He could not hide his emotion, believing now that finally the battle was over and he had won this entire war on his own.

Just then, without warning, he was shoved from behind, falling headfirst into the gunge-filled trench, his rifle falling away. Covered from head to toe in mud and slush, he desperately looked around and found himself surrounded by the mocking eyes and pointing rifles of the enemy, who stood grinning, baring their teeth below their muddy camouflage.

They now held him and, instead of torturing him, they promised freedom if he worked for them. And he, in his delusion, believed them. In his fear, false hope and desperation, the soldier refused to accept that he had been duped. He fell into the arms of the enemy and became a traitor to his people and his cause.

WHO IS THE ONE?

"Right Terry," said Pastor Brimstone, "have you got it?"

Terry, new recruit to the Church of the Only Path to Heaven, smiled back, gormlessly.

"You get into Pakistan, drive to that village, Nabi Paak, and the deliver the true message to those poor Mozlems! I heard they ain't got no Korans up there in the mountain, so this could be one step in our mission to bring the world to the Only Path to Heaven, you understand?"

"Ye-ez Pastor Brimstone."

"You iz one of hundreds of disciples of the Only Path going into Pakistan and India to bring some light to that dark, heathen place!!! You get it?"

"Ye-ez Pastor Brimstone."

"Don't forget the truth Terry!"

"I won't Pastor, sir!"

"Feel the truth, son!"

"I will, Papa, I mean Pastor, sir!"

"Who is the one, Terry?"

Terry stood dumbstruck for a minute.

"I said, who is the one, Terry? Say it!" Pastor Brimstone was locked in a fervent frenzy.

"Who is the one Terry?!" Terry repeated.

"I said: who is the one?! Say it like you mean it son!"

"WHO IS THE ONE?!" Terry screamed, then began to cough.

"THAT'S RIGHT SON, YOU GOT IT, THAT'S WHAT YOU GOTTA SHOW THOSE WRETCHED BROWN SKINS SEARCHING FOR HOPE, SON!!! WHO IS THE ONE?!" He paused.

Terry was still coughing.

"Okay son, you got the spirit and you got the truth, now go git!"

And with that, Terry, still in a fit of coughing was shepherded out of the ministry, deposited on a private plane, filled with disciples of the Only Path.

It wasn't too long until Terry found himself, alone, in Islamabad airport, where another member of the Only Path appeared and quietly guided Terry to an awaiting shining black vehicle. Twelve hours later, after resting and refuelling physically and mentally, Terry reached the bumpy track which led up to a settlement, cradled beneath one of the colossal mountains of the Himalayas, the village, Nabi Paak.

A village, Terry was told, which had become cut off from the outside world, where Korans were no longer read, where even the Taliban would not venture into because of the nature of the people.

What Terry wasn't told was that the Taliban had lost all hope for this place and were not going to waste any valuable gun powder because the people were a bunch of buffoons. The village was in the grip of a rare illness which induced mass memory loss. For the past year, the whole village population had forgotten their culture, their religion and their history. A very strange state of affairs indeed for a village which was once teeming with dervishes, disciples and worshippers. Now the mosques lay empty. Korans were no longer read. The azaan, a forgotten tune. But before he passed away, the holy man of the village had predicted this event would occur, and had instructed the people to inscribe some words into the walls of their houses so that they would not forget. He told them that one day, when they came into trouble, these words would set them free.

Anyway, it was on that fateful day, a Friday, when the people of village all gathered together in the village square outside the mosque, unable to remember why they used to do that. Out of habit, they would all just sit there and talk about their goats, the mountains and whether Asif Zardari was the name of a Bollywood villain.

Suddenly, Terry emerged, dressed in a dark suit, white shirt and his name glistening off his badge from the midday sun.

He stood in front of the villagers, blocking out the sun and, for a moment, they were all dazzled and had to block their eyes.

"Oh sorry." Said Terry, and instead he stood under the shade of a nearby tree.

The villagers could now see him clearly and were at first dumbstruck.

Then suddenly, one shouted out: "Gora hei!"

Now they were awestruck and mumblings of "gora hei!" And "Yei Gora kon hei?" hummed in among the crowd. They sat, ready and savouring what he would say, this white man from beyond.

Terry began: "I am Terry!" His voice seemed to wobble a bit. The villagers looked at each other, rather unimpressed.

"I have come here to tell you the truth!" That was better, an inner strength boomed from his voice. But his audience was still unmoved.

"The truth is," and with that, Terry began to speak of his religion and saviour of the world, in a rather long-winded way it has to be said. And it only took a few minutes for the villagers to start mumbling to each other in frustration:

"Gora paghal hei!" (The white man is crazy!)

"Yei keya kehraha hei?" (What is he talking about?)

"EEDYUT!" (IDIOT)

Poor Terry could see he was losing them when suddenly a memory shone in his head, the parting advice of his mentor, Pastor Brimstone, the truth, the whole truth, the only way to heaven!

"WHO IS THE ONE?!!!"

Terry's voice shook with passion and the sentence seemed to echo around the mountains and even reach the ether.

The villagers first looked at each other, rather confused. But then something strange happened. The light of understanding began to appear on their faces; they all began smiling, some even shed tears. A realisation entered their hearts, like they had found a long lost friend. Terry could see that his words, his true words, were having the right impact. So he shouted it again, this time, raising both arms in the air like a soothsayer.

"WHO IS THE ONE!!!"

The second time seemed to have a rousing impact, for suddenly a villager leapt up in ecstasy and said, strangely in broken English:

"THE WALL! THE WALL! HAZRAT SAAB! HE TOLD US! YOU WRITE: HU IS ONE!!! YOU REMEMBER? HU IS ONE!!!"

This wild utterance set the whole crowd off and they began to chant wildly, tossing their heads to and fro:

"ALLAH HU! ALLAH HU! ALLAH HU! ALLAH HU! ALLAH HU! ALLAH HU! ALLAH HU!"

They all leapt up and carried Terry on their shoulders, hailing him a hero, for he had helped them to get their memories back, their faith back, their Allah back! And up and the down the mountains they went chanting, while Terry just seemed to lap up the attention and let things take their course, looking around, chuckling to himself, "who is the one," with no idea in heaven what they were all chanting about:

"ALLAH HU! ALLAH HU! ALLAH HU! ALLAH HU! ALLAH HU! ALLAH HU! ALLAH HU! ALLAH HU! ALLAH HU!"

THE ROBBERY

"This is a robbery! Everyone put your hands in the air, NOW!"

The large grey-suited man, masked with a brown stocking which made him look like a scarecrow, jumped on the nearest table, pointing his automatic rifle around the bank, as the shrieking employees and customers cowered behind desks.

"I said put your hands in the air! Are you totally thick or something?" He barked aggressively.

Scores of hands now rose to the air, some trembling with intense fear.

"And shut up, if you don't want a bullet through yer brain!"

The shrieking and screaming suddenly stopped.

Two more bulky men materialised behind the first one, similarly dressed and wearing rifles underneath their suits. One of them addressed the terrified crowd.

"First of all, if any of you even think about pressing your alert buttons, I'll put a bullet through your fingers, before you can say the word bank. Do you get me? Anyway, pressing the button won't do much good because we've just switched off the mains of the whole street." With that, he chuckled to himself in sort of a machine gun rattle and carried on: "we are here to take some precious things and then we will be away in a matter of minutes. We do not want to harm anyone, but if you try something stupid or try to act like a hero out of 'Die Hard'," and here he paused and pointed his rifle at the crouching security guards, "you will die...hard!" This time, all three villains laughed aloud, in the same machine gun rattle.

"That was a good one mate," laughed the first robber.

"Oh cheers, Teena," replied the second one. They all seemed to be oblivious about the fact that he had revealed the first robber's name.

The second one continued: "So, my friend here will watch over you, to ensure you don't get up to any shenanigans, while my other colleague and I do our business, and then we will leave you to carry on with your business."

The two robbers left the third one behind with the hostages, while they walked through to the back room. The leader, who had spoken before, brought out a map and pointed at a spot.

"Right, so they should be behind this door to the right." Using the keys they had procured from the manager, they unlocked a large, solid oak door and entered a vast room, filled with hundreds and hundreds of drawers.

"Here they all are!" Said the leader. "Right, let's use the keys the boss gave us. Don't forget his instructions. In and out in ten minutes. Don't forget the tiny specks. "

They pulled out a strange-looking key, from their pockets, extremely thin, like the scales of a fish, scarlet in colour, and shaped like a snake's tongue at the end.

The two men picked a drawer each from different sides of the room. The locks clicked simultaneously and the robbers pulled out the drawers, which were actually, long thin boxes. A mischievous grin appeared on each of their faces. Using the keys again, they unlocked the boxes from above and lifted the lids.

"Wow!" said the leader.

"Jackpot!" exclaimed the other.

"What have you got in yours?"

The leader paused for the moment, and then with an evil smile said, "I got Ramadan fasts...He was swearing and fighting during most of em. What you got in yours?"

"I got sadaqas! Hundreds of them. He told all his mates about them."

They both cackled, wickedly, then producing large folded up bags from inside of their suits, they emptied the contents into the bags.

In a sudden burst of energy, they whizzed around the room like sprites, unlocking the drawers and emptying the contents into their bags, while commenting on what they got.

"Tahleels! Hundreds of them! He looked at porn a few hours afterwards!"

"Three juz of the Quran. Then she told her mate that her mother-in-law was a witch."

"Oh my god, I've hit the jackpot here. Tahajjuds! A whole year of them."

"You lucky devil!"

"He read them for a whole year, but he was also smacking his wife around for a whole year!"

"The boss is gonna be real proud us!" The leader proclaimed.

"Yeah, real proud."

"Can't wait to see that look on his face. He was down in the dumps all last month."

"Yeah, he didn't half give us grief."

"But now that it's Shawwal, he should brighten up."

A few minutes elapsed. The boxes had been emptied, the bags were packed full and the three robbers left the bank like the wind blowing through the trees.

They travelled far from the town, celebrating and savouring the moment that they would present their spoils to the boss.

Suddenly, the leader stopped in his tracks and held his colleagues back.

"Wait, wait!"

"What is it?" The other two enquired.

"We forgot something!"

"No we didn't," the other two protested, "look at the bags, they're packed full of stuff!"

"The specks, they were still in the boxes..."

"What specks?"

"Hating it in your heart, the weakest of iman."

"AAAH!!!"

BANKRUPT

At the Malay stock exchange, one early morning, the managing director of Huwa industries appeared in a dreadful state, with his shirt untucked, his tie hanging wildly around his neck, pacing around, in his bare feet, in a never-ending circle, lamenting:

"I've lost it all...I've missed it...What will he say?"

Nobody disturbed him and just allowed this new, mystery tycoon to make a complete fool of himself in front of his competitors, who were sitting majestically in their booths which gazed down on the stock exchange floor.

A few minutes elapsed. Expecting to see this new guy's stocks plummet to the floor, the MDs of the opposing share companies began rubbing their hands.

But, suddenly, to their utter disbelief, they saw Huwa Industries' shares rocketing way above all of their shares put together!

They stared at the numbers on the vast board then watched this peculiar man continue his circuit and disappear out of sight.

What the hell? They all thought.

The next day, there was the same scenario: the stock exchange; the daily forecast; the MDs ready in their booths. But today, this bright morning, the MD of Huwa industries appeared with his aide, with an air of utter composure and grace.

Conversely, Huwa shares had fallen flat. He had lost millions in dollars. The MDs grinned as they looked at the figures, but then gawked at the composure and grace of the new guy, as he paced around the stock exchange, gazing serenely at the board.

"Right, that's it." Announced one those seated, "Call his aide. I want to know what's going on."

A few moments later, on the floor, the MD's aide felt a tap on the shoulder, heard a whisper in his ear which impelled him to whisper into his own master's ear. The MD on the floor motioned him to accede to the request being made to him.

So when the sharp-looking aide finally reached the pompous men in their leather chairs, staring at him rather contemptuously, one of the MDs piped up:

"Now listen here young man. What the hell is wrong with your boss? Today, his shares have plummeted and he stands there like a god. And yesterday his shares rocketed and he's pacing around like a homeless alcoholic. What on earth is going on?"

The MDs all held their breaths, curious, intrigued. And all the aide could say was this:

"Well, today, my dear sirs, my respected boss managed to wake up for Fajr prayers."

CAPTIVATION

Since its sudden appearance one morning onto the Arts corridor decades ago, the *Captivation* painting, a wonderful view of the countryside through a gigantic window perhaps in a stately home, had mystified academics, students and visitors to the university.

No signature or receipt could be found except for the title, which was etched into the wooden frame. The premises manager, then, finally attributed the picture to an anonymous donor or to a hidden artist of the university who wanted to decorate the corridors with their work, and if the painting was not of the highest quality the manager would have ordered its removal.

At first glance, this work of art would have pleased the eye because of the finesse and fluidity of the brush strokes and the perfect balance of the shading. Only when people glanced at the bottom corner, next to the meadow gate, would they raise an eyebrow and look again. A distinct, blank outline of an upright human being, a man, interrupted the space between the gate and the pathway leading to it, spoiling the atmosphere of the painting.

This shape was not graffiti because it retained the same texture as the rest of the scene and it did not prove the work was unfinished because the outline had been carefully drawn in to resemble the form of a man. And those who maintained the work was surrealist art were forced to admit that no apparent symbolism could be found in the figure; it looked more like a spirit. This ghost-like blank figure gave the picture the resemblance of one of those classic haunted photographs which when developed had picked out an apparition.

The mystery of the figure was destined to persist as the artist or donor never came forward with an explanation. However, a terrifying development was to take place when an addition was unexpectedly made or one might say when the picture was finally completed which a horrified cleaner discovered, one wonderful morning in the present day.

The day before the discovery, a uniformed deliveryman entered the university carrying a box full of stationery for the admin office.

The staff explained how the man appeared to be in a trance, as he placed the box in the office and asked for signatures. One lady in the office mentioned that the man's expressionless face and distant stare reminded her of people she had witnessed being hypnotised in a show.

Subsequently, the man's behaviour made the admin staff very uncomfortable and an alerted security guard kept careful watch over the man's movements. Then, as the deliveryman left, he told the guard blankly that he was going to use the toilet on the first floor along the Arts corridor. This statement shocked the guard, as the man could not have known the location of the toilet if he had never been to the university before. But the guard assented, not wanting to provoke a confrontation, and as the man left him, the guard instructed the office to call the police because he was sure this man was planning something, perhaps terrorism. But before the guard could realise, he found that the man had already reached the stairs and was rapidly climbing up to the first floor. The guard flew after him to ensure he had the man in his sights but when the guard got to the Arts corridor he stood dumbstruck.

The deliveryman had vanished. And he was not found in the toilets, the rooms along the corridor, and after phone calls from the delivery company, the arrival of the police and an entire search of the university, not anywhere in the building. After that the deliveryman was never seen again in the physical world.

It was only the next morning during the glorious sunshine, when the sunlight beautifully lit the corridors, that a cleaner, while dusting the paintings along the Arts corridor, made a nightmarish discovery. The *Captivation* painting had been violated. The apparition-like figure had been inhabited. Enmeshed and fitting perfectly into the outline, comically shrunken and with a petrified stare stood the deliveryman.

THE GRASS

"All things hang like a drop of dew
Upon a blade of grass".

W B Yeats

A lush and fertile patch of grass shivered in the breeze, sighing blissfully. Fully exposed to the benevolent sun and enriched by the timely monsoons, the grass grew to a staggering height, accommodating countless creatures great and small. Nothing, so it seemed, could curtail its life-force; nothing could obstruct the sun or the rain replenishing it. The grass was suffused with a rich and deep shade of green, so much so that just to look upon it brought relief to hearts, just to hear its whispers in the wind brought tranquility to troubled minds.

But times changed; people changed; natures evolved; subtle ideas began to fester. A snake from beyond settled in the grass, twisting its coils between the blades and whispering subtle suggestions to the very roots of the green sea.

Time elapsed; the snake slithered away, but its ideas had taken root; the grass was spellbound. Now the blessings of the sun and the rain were mistaken for rights; fortune was misinterpreted as certainty. Although the sun continued to beam its rays upon everything and the rain still tumbled down, the grass had grown thick in its own delusions of grandeur and its right to the blessings from above.

Without it realising, the roots below turned a sickly yellow and each blade of grass began to smell rank and rotten to the core.

Suddenly, humans arrived, with their hulky, moving machinery, dumping all their garbage and rubble from their developments, covering the grass with a dense layer of suffocating trash. A vast cloud of stifling dust rose after an immense vehicle unloaded mounds of dirt on the once green patch.

Now the grass felt this calamity spreading through its veins; each blade flattened by the grey flood. Its heart lamented as it lay deep beneath the rubble, divorced from the light above, cut off from the rain. Its blissful sighs had now turned into smothered cries for deliverance. It had not anticipated this catastrophe and now, flattened in the darkness, it confounded the snake it had listened to so enrapt, and it cried for the sun to reach it once again, for the rain to touch the tips of its blades.

So the sun still shone; the rains still fell; the earth still revolved. Desperate and humbled, the grass cried out from the darkness. Time healed. The sun's rays slowly penetrated the ground, the rain drops crept through the earth.

Until one day, out of all the toxic mass and trash, something stood out proudly from the earth, like an outstretched index finger, like a spirit awakened, touched by the sun's rays, refreshed by a lingering drop of dew: a blade of grass.

THE DELIRIOUS DERALING OF
MULLAH KHAN'S DE-RADICALIZATION

Mullah Khan, the irrepressible zealot and his sons, had been forced to attend the first ever de-radicalization programme, sanctioned and championed by none other than the British Prime Minister himself, Davis Cameroon. Khan and his sons were deemed social menaces with their firebrand Islamism, their desperation for Britain to become an Islamic state, their adoration for the self-styled caliph of ISIS, Abu Bakr Al Baghdadi, and also for their failed mission to blow up a pig farm in Dudley with an explosive that they named "Kufr-Killer".

So Cameroon, fresh from an election victory and smug as a bug, cosied up to a few decent moderate ex-Islamists, re-read his copy of "Islam For Idiots", by Robert Spencer, and subsequently announced that British Muslims were ineffectual in dealing with their scriptural anachronisms and their bad apples:

"I shall embark on plucking out these bad apples myself," he proclaimed, shaking his fist, "drill inside, find the Islamist worm and then crush it, leaving behind a wholesome, moderate, red, empire apple. Or golden delicious if you prefer." He chuckled at his own joke at this point in the press conference.

So Mullah Khan and sons were the first to be purged of their Islamism. This new, governmental initiative involved ex-radicals working with the family, encouraging introspection, victim impact analysis and embracing the universal values of love and peace.

And things looked pretty dire from the very start.

Mullah Khan arrived at the centre, a stately home in the middle of the Chiltern hills, clad in parachute-style, light blue salwar qameez, a pair of white Reeboks and a green baseball hat, sporting the Pakistan flag. His beard hung below him like a cascade of black, candy-floss. His eyes bulged in their sockets, dark and terrible. His sons, triplets, all in their late teens and basically teenage versions of their dad, all jumped out of their dad's grey Toyota Yaris with the nifty little spoiler and Islam4UK stickers in the back window.

The manager and coordinator, Gary Juggan, a withered-looking Southerner, skinny as a flint in a navy blue suit and Union-Jack tie, came to greet the family outside the centre, pleasantly offering his hand to Mullah Khan.

"KUFR!" Exclaimed Mullah Khan, pointing at Gary's face.

"SHIRK!" Cried his son, Mullah Shah, pointing at Gary's tie.

"BIDA!" Shrieked the next son, Mullah Jang, pointing at Gary's mobile phone.

"NIFAAQ!" Shouted Mullah Hamza, gesticulating at the entire building.

Gary Juggan looked rather bemused at first, but laughed it all off.

"Sorry," he began politely, "but I don't seem to follow you…"

He was interrupted very quickly with the same chorus:

"KUFR!" Cried Mullah Khan.

"SHIRK!" Cried Mullah Shah.

"BIDA!" Growled Mullah Jang.

"NIFAAQ!" Yelled Mullah Hamza.

Juggan now began scratching his head, completely flummoxed, but he thought it would be better to lead the family into the centre to get processed.

"OK," he said, very slowly, "all of you," pointing to the man and his sons, "you follow me here…"

A moslamic volcano erupted.

"KUFR!"

"SHIRK!"

"BIDA!"

"NIFAAQ!"

Then all four of them started punching their fists in the air and shouting slogans:

"DEATH TO THE QUEEN! DEATH TO THE WEST! SHE'S AS DRUNK AS GEORGIE BEST!"

That day, as the family were processed and settling in the centre, Juggan sought some solace from the newly appointed consultant on the six-figure salary instituted by Cameroon, Najeed Mawaz.

"Najeed," stated Gary, as the two observed the family, behind the screen, in their large room, setting up their beds to face Mecca and sticking ISLAM4UK stickers all over the place, "what are those words they keep saying whenever they see me?"

"Well Gary," started Najeed, pleased at the opportunity to educate his boss, "kufr is the Arabic word for unbelief, shirk is the word for idolatry, bida is for misguiding innovations and finally nifaaq is the word for hypocrisy."

"Oh," said Gary, hesitating and looking worried, "I see…So basically, I am the walking personification of the infidel for them."

"No, no. Don't worry," reassured Najeed, patting Gary on the shoulder, "once they've been with me, they'll be fine; just you watch. I am sure I will learn something from them as well. They're only human at the end of the day."

So, the next day, the family was summoned into a well-lighted, modern seminar room. They each took a seat and waited. There were biscuits, jammie dodgers, bourbons and chocolate chip cookies scattered on plates before them, with piping hot tea and milk.

They all responded with, "KUFR! SHIRK! BIDA! NIFAAQ!" But then they started tucking into the beverages and biscuits with wide smiles on their faces.

"Bloody kafirs make lovely biscuits though," remarked one of the brothers.

"The red circle in the middle is a right bida! But tastes lovely!" Said another.

"Stupid cookies get too soft and soggy like a mushrik!" The third complained.

"BURP!" Went Mullah Khan, after slurping on some tea, and downing a whole plate of bourbons.

Suddenly, a sharp-looking gentleman entered the room. He was dressed in a Calvin Klein, grey, fitted suit, white shirt without tie, a smooth face, interrupted by a cool grey goatee, thick grey curls, well-groomed, milk chocolate face.

"As salaamu alaykum, my dear, dear brothers, my name is Najeed."

The four stopped chomping and slurping and looked at the new arrival suspiciously, who had just parked himself on the chair opposite them.

"Look, I just want to start by saying that I am not here representing the government. I am here as a true brother to you in Islam. I am your akhee."

The four looked at each other stone-faced and then back at Najeed. He twitched slightly.

"Okay, so look. The first thing we are going to do today is to make introductions. I will start. My name is Najeed. I used to be a fighter for the Islamo-Liberation front and I was imprisoned by the regime in Blaggakisstan. I know what it means to be angry. I know what it means to want the West to suffer. I know what it means to desire for laws according to the Quran and Sunna." He stopped and briefly observed his listeners to ascertain any impact. They still sat stone-faced. He coughed slightly and carried on:

"So I know how it feels my brothers. But in time, I learned that hatred and violence is the opposite of Islam. I learned that the things they taught me to hate, like democracy, like women's liberation, like homosexuality, like McDonald's and the Queen, all these things I once hated, I learned in time, that actually, they are all the creation of Allah. Allah is vast and inviting. Allah is one but Allah is for all. So that's me, do you want to go next Mullah Khan?"

Mullah Khan folded his arms impressively so that his wistful beard rested on his wrists.

"Sons, you go first."

Mullah Shah piped up first, "listen to this you walking piece of nifaq, with your bida beard and your shirky talk, we don't have to listen to you."

"Yeah, you're not our akhee, Mr Bida! You are just full of kufr!" Mullah Jang added.

"Now hang on!" Protested Najeed.

"No, you hang on," Chimed in Mullah Hamza, "we will not rest, we will not stop, we will listen only to the power and the might of the caliph of Islam who dwells in Iraq called Baghdadi, and we will never rest until all the kufr, shirk, bida and nifaaq are cleared from the world. There is no God but the tawheed of Allah!"

Then the three triplets began chanting:

"I'D RATHER HAVE TAWHEED! INSTEAD OF NAJEED!

GIVE US TAWHEED! REJECT NAJEED!"

After that meeting, Najeed swiftly visited Gary.

"I think we're gonna have to get some help with these guys. I've never seen anything like it!"

And during that week, Gary and Najeed, first enlisted the help of trained counsellors. After two days, they all quit.

Then they brought in the hardnuts from MI5 to try the hard way.

"You've tried your de-radicalization," muttered the suited agents to Gary and Najeed, "now let us try some rather unorthodox methods…"

But the agents couldn't even get anywhere close to the father and his sons without being shouted down as, "KUFR! SHIRK! BIDA! NIFAAQ!"

After just half an hour of being subjected to the constant bombardment, the MI5 agents were beginning to crack and even Gary and Najeed were noticing it:

"I can't get those words out of my head…" Remarked one of the agents, haunted.

"No more kufr. No more shirk." The second agent began mumbling under his breath as he left the building.

Incidentally, two years later, the two aforementioned agents were found in Raqqa, Syria, slurping on mint tea while shouting to the camera, "KILL THE PORK!"

In fact, the whole centre, the admin staff, the cooks and the guards were all falling under the spell of Mullah Khan and his sons. Until, to the horror of Najeed and Gary, they heard choruses of the following chants echoing in the kitchen, the admin office and the bar: "NO MORE BIDA! NO MORE SHIRK! KILL THE KUFR! JOIN ISIS!"

Najeed was forced to admit his failure to Cameroon, who had to keep this all quiet, so he had a group of trained killers, like Jason Bourne, execute all involved in this project.

Mullah Khan and his sons were shipped off to Raqqa by direct orders of prime minister, Davis Cameroon, whose aides remarked was having nightmares of himself dressed in a turban, shouting, "KILL THE MUSHRIKS!"

Mullah Khan and his sons were treated like royalty when they entered the ISIS stronghold and were given private audience with none other than the self-styled caliph himself, Abu Bakr Al Baghdadi. But when he entered into the room, it is reported that Baghdadi was carrying a mobile phone and was wearing jeans, to which the Khan family responded with a resounding: "KUFR! SHIRK! BIDA! NIFAAQ!"

After some minutes, the caliph could not take it anymore, and he ordered for them to be sent away to the furthest border possible. Some say afterwards Baghdadi was found many days later, after being reported missing, with a circle of dervishes by the Tigris, wailing and crying: "save me Allah! Oh save me!"

Mullah Khan ended up with his sons, on the border of a well-known kingdom.

"Dad, where are we?" They asked.

Mullah Khan's eyes welled with tears and a grateful smile appeared on his face:

"Sons, Allah has brought us to a special kingdom. This is the realm where we will find no kufr, no bida, no Shirk and no nifaaq! WE HAVE ARRIVED IN THE ISLAMIC KINGDOM OF SAUDI ARABIA MY SONS! LEAD US TO THE KING!!!

THE OLD MAN
AND HIS CHILDREN

*The greatest trick the devil plays on man is
to make him believe he is free.*

Far away in the hills, there lived this big, proud old man, with his wife and many young children. This man was larger than life, extremely generous and caring to his dependants, but at times he could be cruel and tyrannical. Consequently his children would flee when rage filled him and his wife would weep when anger swelled in his eyes. This old man led his family the way he saw fit, and for many a year lived like a king of his own little world.

His kingdom was the land which lay around his cabin, where he grew some vegetables and survived on some livestock that he kept. As a family they were fairly poor, and their methods of living were crude, but they hardly ever starved, and such was their country and land, that rain was never scarce and their limited land and animals hitherto dependable.

The old man had links with another family, who dwelled in this vast landscape of rolling hills, forests, glens, lakes and meadows. His closest neighbours were the distance of a few days of walking and they were rather different. The children, being slightly older than his, were harder to control and demanded their say in how things were run around place. The old man had realised that the children of this household had stood up to the tyranny of their father and now they and their mother held sway over the household. This factor did not please the old man, for he wished that his own family did not come into contact with the outside world. But the old man depended on this neighbour. They liked his vegetables, which did not grow in their fields, and their hay and grass was particularly appetising for his animals. The grass and hay in his field was not as copious or healthy. This was why the old man had to make regular trips, swapping his goods for their goods, eventually becoming a close ally of the father and a friend to his children. Deep down, he knew that as his own children grew, his power would slowly slip away just like his neighbour. Still he made a point of not allowing his family to accompany him on any of his trips.

An added problem in time for both families was their aging resources. The old man and his neighbour faced some difficult times. With dwindling livestock, and without a sign of growth, they went in search of other families, who they surmised lived far to the south, so that they could try to offer them vegetables and hay in return for goods.

To their amazement, after many days travelling, they found another family, who had darker skin and who possessed land rich with fruits and animals they had never seen. This new family was amazed to see these two old and strong white fellows, with their amazing vegetables and hay, with their charming voices and authoritarian air. So the old man and his neighbour started trading supplies with them, thereafter, taking the long trips out there from time to time, swapping their vegetables and hay for their exotic fruits and animals.

Until one day, the two neighbours had a wicked idea. They had gained the trust of the head of this family, who led his tribe much like the old man and his neighbour. Moreover, the wife and children also trusted the new men well. Knowing this, the old man conjectured to his neighbour, that if he taught the wife and the children to stand up to their father secretly, he could use it to his own advantage. Their father would surely come to him for help, as the darker man had become attached to the old man and his friend.

And this is exactly what occurred. After some clever and cunning words to the rest of the family, the old man and his neighbour saw the dark-skinned father coming to them and sharing his problems. And behind his back, the old man promised the wife and children that he would convince their father to give them more respect and freedom in return for good treatment. Amidst all his manipulations, the old man had also made them believe how much they all needed his vegetables and his neighbour's hay. They all trusted the old man so much, that they even gave more of their fruits and animals in trade for the few the vegetables and hay they brought on each trip. A time came, when the dark-skinned children and their parents now depended on the old man for survival, because they had granted him authority and rights over their fruits.

Time passed. The old man's family was growing older in age, more aware of their own strength, but completely unaware of their father's exploit beyond the hills. The old man fumed because now he had made his house bigger with the goods he had attained from the dark-skinned ones, and ensured there was plenty of food and supplies for his wife and children. Despite his excellent providence, he knew his children would eventually grow older and overcome his power. He hated the thought of losing his way.

So he had another plan. To ensure his power would always reign, even without his dependants realising. He made a pact with the fathers all around the area, who he and his neighbour had discovered through time, to share in his secret, for they all faced the same dilemmas, of their children growing up and their wives losing their fear. The old man made trips around all these houses, spellbinding the growing children with his stories of far and dangerous places, instilling confidence that they one day would rule like their fathers, but also making them fear what was outside with his magical presentations. They believed him and hung on his every word. Likewise, he hired his own neighbour to enter his own domain, and make friendships with his own wife and children, and in a similar way, charm them with stories of power and fearful places.

Eventually, the wives and the growing children were certain of two things: that one day, they would have more power to decide their own fates, and also, the world was a fearful place, which was treacherous to travel and explore.

Time moved on. The old man and his neighbour found more dark-skinned families to exploit, which made him and his neighbours richer. His children continued to grow, until one day, they rose forth, full of power and strength, announcing that their father would no longer rule the household, but they would, and any decision would be made fairly and through consultation. No more biased, one-sided decisions from their father. It was a sensational moment in their lives. The adrenalin rush of freedom intoxicated them. And at this moment, they all looked on at the sad face of their father, who now saw his own children following the trend of all the other children around them. The old world was dead.

But now a new order had begun. The children felt proud and free, that they now ruled their own lands, and they held sway over their rich and well-resourced home. Instead of their father ordering them around to do the chores, and get supplies, now they all did it themselves, and they promoted their mother to the status of a queen, while their father had the role of the retired leader who now had to blend into their shadows.

But, amazingly, they did not stop their father from his little trips beyond the hills. And likewise, the other children from all the other households allowed their own fathers on their trips abroad. They had no desire to find out what lie beyond their world. So engrossed had they become with the power they held in their hands, that they had no care or concern about the others houses and what was going on there. They still knew nothing of the fact the very riches and prosperity they now ruled over, had been gained by their father's exploitation of the dark-skinned families down south.

Fear and hate began to rise. The dark-skinned children grew to hate the old man and his neighbour, and no longer liked their visits but resented them. They had become poor and weak. They had heard of the riches of the pale skinned children far to the north and how the dark-skinned families around had become impoverished. Bitterness grew in these children. Anger. They had been duped. Their own parents were powerless to act. So the children decided to embark on a reign of terror.

After much trouble and pain, the dark-skinned children found the household of the old man, and began to break its windows and kill their animals, which had once been theirs. The children of the old man, horrified, disgusted, charged out with their pitch forks, fighting off the dark-skinned children, cursing them. They had never spoken to these children before only heard of their barbarism from their father, and decided very quickly that they were evil and a threat to their way of life. So they attacked these foreigners in order to protect their own land and resources. The dark-skinned children were filled with so much hate, that they did not want to speak to the white children to reveal the reason they had become so wretched. They thought these children were the cause of their own suffering. Defeated and dejected the hapless children fled in ignominy.

As these events unfolded, the old man and his neighbour sat back, smiling at the outcome. And as time elapsed, they watched their children, now growing older, holding their regular meetings where everyone had a say about what was to be done. And they chuckled at the way the children all had to put a cross on a piece of wood and place it in a box, which was then counted, and the person with the most crosses would become the leader, or his or her idea would be followed.

"Do you see how wonderful it is to be free!" One of the children said: "We are masters of our own destiny!"

But the old man's two eldest children, a boy and girl, held back and watched the proceedings with an air of shock and sickness. They had followed their father, despite the dangers, to the other houses, to the houses in the south and they had seen what was there. The conspiracy, the poverty, the dependence and the debts the dark-skinned ones owed to their father. And to their horror, the children had realised, that all the comfort and convenience that there was in their own house, had been built upon the exploitation of the other families down south. They suddenly realized why the dark-skinned kids hated them so much. They also realised how the families of the south still depended on them for subsistence. It angered and chilled them both, down to the very marrow in their bones. But the horrifying thing was, there was nothing they could do about it, and in reality, despite the good system they had set up in the home, the voting, the cooperation, they were not really free. They had been duped by their old father.

After much soul-searching, the two eldest settled with this: they decided to live with the guilt and make the best of their lives as much as they could. For ignoring was better than facing up to the truth. The only thing they would do to help the dark-skinned ones was spare some goods each month, and offer them as charity once they were sure the dark-skinned ones would not attack them anymore.

The old man watched his children, playing around and shouting orders, while smoking his pipe, filled with tobacco from the dark-skinned ones, which could not possibly grow on his fields. His smile was wide, for he knew, when he would eventually kick the bucket, there would be two more people to inherit his amazing charade.

And this is what he told his two eldest children, when they returned home that first time from the dark lands, forlorn and knowing the truth: "The greatest lie that the devil plays on mankind is to make him believe he is free."

ABOUT THE AUTHOR

Novid Shaid is an English teacher from the UK, who has taught in various secondary schools for over thirteen years. His first published work is the novel, *The Hidden Ones*. He shares short stories and poems on his website, www.novid.co.uk, and has written a play called *"The War, the Lift and the Separatists"*.